The Life and Times of Allen Court

MeShawn DeBerry

The Life and Times of Allen Court

The Life and Times of Allen Court

ISBN 978-1-41965-052-9
Second Printing March, 2008
Library of Congress 2008903201

Printed in the United States by Morris Publishing
3212 East Highway 30
Kearney, NE 68847
1-800-650-7888

Meshawn Deberry

I give thanks to God first and foremost, my grandparents and all the people who helped along in the process. Thank You.

PROLOGUE:
1984

"How can things change if we don't?" Elder Court said aloud, he stared boldly out the windshield. His son could not answer.

The boy had his eyes locked onto the black forty-four magnum underneath the tape deck. Elder repeated the question as the boy looked over to another gun; a chrome cased twenty-five within a brown leather holster. The silver Cadillac sped around the neighboring corners so fast the car from the outside appeared to bend.

Elder Court glanced fiercely over at a group of crack heads that were leering at his passing car.

Elder continued driving. "Some of those people we just passed are now known as dopeheads, dope fiends. But it ain't that simple. I know some of them as friends, someone else knows them as an uncle, or father and so on." Elder paused for a moment for his message to come through. He opted for a statement. "Son, don't judge people to hard. Let them be who they are and eventually you will see more of what is true about them and yourself. I can't stop the game or some of what you are gonna face while you are in it; but what I can do is give you some awareness."

"Say your name, son?" Elder Court's voice boomed with authority.

"Allen Court." The boy told him.

"How old are you?"

"I'm five." Allen said. "What's in a name? It can put you in some category , it can size you up. But don't you ever let someone else box you in. What are you going to be when you grow up?"

Allen paused he could not answer the question. His eyes were focused on the weapons beneath him.

"Whatever you do, do your own thing." Elder Court interjected, breaking his son's silence. "Take the good of the people around you and learn how to live your life.."

Allen looked out the car window. He looked at the passing kids on the street.

"Church Road."

"I know people who spent their whole lives on this street. It's a whole world out there for us but all we get to see is the same thing! We need more economic opportunities, more businesses more libraries and schools in our community.

Allen continued to stare out the window. Thinking of playing catch with his cousins, feeling very content, to stay upon that street.

"I know I put a lot on you in a short time. You know, I have to talk to you like you was a grown man, already. Black boys have to grow up fast. Sometimes, too fast"

The Cadillac turned into the parking lot where Elder owned an arcade, next door, was the liqueur store he also owned. Elder leaned his long legs out of the car; Allen hurried to unlock the door trying to move as fast as his father. They stepped from the door, two men walked by to talk with Elder. Allen stood in admiration in how his father towered over the people around him. Allen's admiration came from the seriousness that his father could captivay at times and how just as easily a smile could suddenly appear across his fathers face in the same breath. Nevertheless people circled around the man like he was a solar system of his own. Elder went to the trunk of his car; he grabbed a small duffel bag then headed inside the store.

The Life and Times of Allen Court

A young girl flirted with Elder, he nonchalantly brushed her off. She then turned her attention to Allen; leaning over pinching his cheek.

"Ooh, you're gonna be so handsome when you grow up," The oval-faced woman blurted out.

"Leave my son alone," Elder said smiling. "Allen, come on, get what you want."

Allen turned his attention to gathering enough candy to last him two weeks. He gorged himself on penny candy as his father counted money from the cash register.

Later in the day, after the sun set, Elder took Allen downstairs into the rickety basement. A rusty pipe dripped constantly, dotting a trail to a solid black safe standing in the middle of a wet concrete floor. Elder turned the combination of the safe with exact precision, exposing towers of bills in front of his son.

Elder took the money from the duffel bag that had earlier and placed it into the safe. Allen could not see how much it was, although he bent a crook in his neck trying to look.

The two walked back up to the stairs, stopping along the way. Elder grabbed a soda for Allen, and a bottle of gin for himself. As the two sit below the moonlit sky, Allen contemplated the distance between himself and the heavens. Allen asked suddenly, "What would happen if you shot the moon?" Elder laughed aloud, nearly spilling his drink.

"You'll miss, it's too far away. Gravity pulls on the bullet, making it fall to the earth. Gravity pulls all things downward to earth."

"Me and you?" Allen asked, still looking at the moon.

"You, me, and everything else in this small planet." Elder leaned over and hugged his son. "But on a different note. Even though there are things that may come and try to pull you down don't you ever give up. You can make something good happen with your life. Come on, let me take you home."

When they pulled up to the house, Allen noticed a new face to the neighborhood. A young girl stood in the middle of the yard with an older man. The older gentleman was speaking with Allen's grandfather. Elder said goodbye as Allen was leaving the car.

"It didn't work out between your mother and I, but you have to stay strong and listen to what she tells you. Take care of yourself," Elder opened the door for him.

Allen shut the car door behind him. His attention focused on his new neighbors. The older man began to speak with Allen.

"Hi, my name is Maleek," the old man said before pointing to a girl around Allen's age. "This here is my granddaughter, Cynthia."

"Smile. Say something," His aunt Veal teased him as she walked in the yard. Allen smiled and said hello.

"I like your bike…" Cynthia said. Allen smiled proudly; looking over his star-spangled Evil Knievel bike.

"…But, I don't need the training wheels," the girl finished. The smile left Allen's face.

"I don't need 'em. They're for my little cousin," he lied. "You don't have to ride with me, anyway." He said angrily.

"I don't need to. I have my own bike," She told him, frankly. "But, I still like yours."

"I don't think I like you. And I hope my momma don't make me sit next to you; when we go to school." The girl looked at him, saddened by what he said. He felt an instant regret. "I'm sorry. I don't really mean that." Allen handed her some candy that he had gotten from his fathers store trying to make a peace offering. She smiled and accepted.

7

"My favorite," Cynthia said, Maleek laughed at them.

"You two should get along well together." Maleek said to them. "I have a feeling that you will."

Allen shrugged his shoulders and walked into the house. His aunt called him, "You going to see your baby brother? I saw him."

"You did!" Allen smiled. "He's only two weeks old." Allen told her.

"You just came back from seeing your daddy?" His aunt asked. Allen shook his head, yes.

"What did he give you?"

Allen pulled out a handful of penny candy and handed some to her. A few pieces fell on the floor

"Ahh man, dang."

"His aunt burst out laughing, his preaching uncle, thought he had overheard what Allen had said.

"Hhmmph, just like his daddy." He said in a huff. "Cussing already, and at five."

"Boy, I tell you. Boy, I tell you!" Kicking his feet out in a shuffle, "There is some history there."

Allen trudged by, trying to keep the attention off him. His preaching uncle could be heard speaking loudly, while his grinning uncles; tossed down silver 18-ounce cans of Schlitz malt liqueur. Allen walked by as his preaching uncle shouted.

"That boy got some roots. Ain't no way in the world, an Anderson and a Court, should be mixed. But here he is, right there in the flesh."

"Yup, there he is." Allen's grinning uncle Teddy would say in response pulling the boy underneath his arm.

"Take a sip, but don't tell your momma." He rested the can to Allen's' mouth.

Allen pulled the can up to his lips and grimaced at the bitter taste of the beer. But, before long he was stumbling around the record player, dancing as his sinning uncles grinned and his preaching uncle preached.

"Just like his daddy." The preacher would say shaking his head, leaving the room in frustration.

Allen did not know what was wrong. Teddy picked him up.

"Allen, don't worry about what that nigga say." His uncle spit out.

"Speak the truth some can, living the truth, that's another thing." Teddy hugged him "Now it's late, so you better go to bed before your mother comes out here and get in our ass for letting you drink this beer."

Allen sulked as he walked to his room. He stopped by his door to kick off his shoes. Then he sneaked around the corner to his grandmother's door. He walked in.

His grandmother kneeled over her bed, silently praying. Her small, quiet body and long black hair drowned out the commotion that was going on in the other rooms. Allen walked over to her. He could smell the sweet jasmine fragrance coming from his grandmothers' hair. He waited at her shoulder for what seemed like an eternity, until he could no longer bare the silence.

"Grandmamma." Allen whispered.

Silence.

"Grannie?" He tugged at the shoulder of her light blue nightgown trying to get her attention.

He waited for what was the rest of forever until she broke her own solitude. She turned to face him with an open smile.

"Yes, Allen."

"Can I pray with you?"

She nodded slowly, grabbing his hands and clasping them close together. She continued kneeling when Allen bent down with her. They began to say the words in unison.

"*Now I lay me down to sleep, I pray the Lord my soul to keep. And if I should die, before I wake, I pray the Lord, my soul to take. Amen.*"

His grandmother walked over to her dresser drawer and picked up her Bible. The book she read from was so large; it could barely fit into Allen's hands open. Allen would try to read for himself, wanting to understand everything he could. He gazed at the pictures, and then looked to his grandmother.

"The words I believe. These pictures, I don't."

His grandmother said, leaned over to kiss him.

"I'm gonna go to bed now," Allen said. He slid off the bed, his bare feet making a light sound after hitting the smooth tile floor.

"Goodnight, Grandmamma."

"Goodnight."

He walked out of her room and silently pulled the door shut. He walked into his room.

"Did you see that new girl?" His uncle Craig asked.

"Yeah, I saw her." He tried to play it off, climbing into his bed.

"She might become your future wife," Craig said.

"She doesn't like me." He hid under the covers.

"Wait until the future." Craig told him.

"The future?" He asked. "I don't know what the future will be?"

"Look over there. We got some new books," Craig pointed to books on a dresser.

Allen jumped off the bed and lifted up one of the editions from a set of twelve books with similar binding. "What are these?" he asked.

"Some encyclopedias that old man, Maleek, had gave me. I took them just to be nice; but I don't know if

I will use them much. You can look at them if you want."

Allen had already started to leaf through the pages of a book. He brushed his hands over three of the encyclopedia volumes. He flipped rapidly through the pages. After a few minutes of this, his uncle became annoyed.

"Put them books down. Why you acting like you can read?"

"I can read." Allen said focused on the book.

"It don't matter anyway. You need to go to bed."

"Can I look at one more?" He pointed to one book along the floor.

"Allen, you can have all the time you want tomorrow. Right now we have to sleep," Craig told him.

"Good night, Allen."

"Good night."

Chapter 1
Year 2000 Reset

"Wake up, wake up." Allen thought as he sat in the airport terminal. He looked around and watched as a plane left the runway in front of him. ""I'm all grown up. Twenty one years old and my first flight. So many things have happened in the last few years." He thought.

Allen stood up; over six foot tall he had filled out over the years. Broad shouldered and strong. His face, long and lean; he turned around looking for the airport dining area.

The Life and Times of Allen Court

'Some things I still haven't been able to get completely over. My pops disappearing on me when I was eleven left me feeling alone. He took a trip west and never was heard from again. Rumors that he may have been killed or got locked up floated around. I may never know the truth." Allen confided. "my heart was filled with anger for a while, some parts of my teenage years. I developed this attitude I can't shake. As far as I'm concerned things change but people stay the same. Why get attached to anybody when they end up leaving you when you need them. Elder didn't leave behind much when it came to money but he did let me know to conserve what I had when I could. Those pieces of advice over the years have worked out nicely. In the last three years I saved up nearly nine grand just from the side jobs I been working while in school. Still, I feel like I raised myself between the streets, sports, school and books. A different combination was the key to unlock this dream.'

Allen looked at a travel magazine someone had left in the seat beside him.

"I use to read about historical places around the world, famous people, I use to wonder what it would be like to see some. Maybe now I will get the chance. The only person I ever shared these thoughts with was with Cynthia. We both kept the same books, read the same stories over the years and compared ideas to the meanings behind the stories." He closed his eyes and saw her for a moment. Long black hair to her shoulders, soft brown eyes and cinnamon colored skin she had grown up, tall and beautiful.

"Cynthia was the one who helped me. She sent me information about exchange programs that I could participate in. Eventually, we both got accepted. She was placed in the American University of Cairo in Egypt. Congratulations! Me, the University of Jyvaskyla, Finland." He chuckled for a moment. "It's a real talent to make the most out of any situation." He thought cynically. "My major is in Sociology and I minor in Chemistry. I should make this trip an independent experiment in social exchange. Real places, real people. Going to school oversees wasn't part of my pedigree, too much into roaming the streets. But now I'm glad to be able to take this chance. Two of my best friends, my aces passed away this year. Chris and Jay. Messed me up for a while. If I can make, it's like, they made it too."

A young married couple walked by breaking Allen from his thoughts. He looked them over thinking back to a time he had last seen Cynthia.

"It's been about a year. She's been my friend since childhood. It started to look like it would turn into something more. We went to different schools but always kept in touch. I spent a weekend with her and it almost went to the next level. I returned back to my school thinking we could stay together. It didn't happen. She started seeing someone else and I decided to let it go. I put all that emotion, all those feelings behind me, find something new. Now we're both taking this chance, but in two different places. I don't see how it can come together. At least; not now."

Allen looked to his right and noticed a small pizza shop. He asked the man behind the counter for a cheese slice. The man had a smile on his face as he handed back Allen his change. .

"Waiting. Most things in life are waiting," The cashier said. Allen looked at the man for a moment, curious about what he meant.

"Waiting?" Allen repeated."What do you mean?"

"If you think about it," the cashier wiped down the clear, white counter, "most things in life are waiting."

Allen realized the double meaning within his phrase.

The Life and Times of Allen Court

"Where are you going? You're obviously are going somewhere," the man asked him.

"I'm going to this country in Scandinavia called Finland." Allen told him.

"That is where I am from!" The man said with a smile. Allen was unmoved. The man began to explain himself.

"Waiting is all apart of patience. I learned this while in the army. My platoon was stationed near the border of Russia. We would have to dig a hole in ice and cover ourselves up and wait until other people in our company came to relieve us. Sometimes, we would have to be there for many, many hours. We would have to wait for the order to move out. Over time, I learned to become patient, because it was the wisest choice."

"And how does this relate to me," Allen asked?

"When you are about to go somewhere, you spend most of your time waiting to get there. Then, once you're there; you spend most of your time waiting to get back."

"Like I am now. I'm waiting to leave this place to go somewhere else." Allen took a slight pause. "I get it. Most things in life are waiting."

"Yes," the former soldier laughed.

"Well, I am here waiting right now, so if you don't mind I'm gonna wait here, for my flight."

"I don't close down until later, take your time." He began to wipe down the counter once more.

Allen nodded and walked to his bags. He slowly turned over the statement in his mind. The term 'waiting' had two meanings for him. "The concept that the soldier tried to explain was so simple that it became confusing.

"How much of my own life have I taken for granted?" He asked himself. "I'm going to make something happen to realize my goals. It's all out there

for me. I just have to be willing to get it. Be aware," he
told himself.

"These hours in between my destination can
teach me just as much as my actual arrival." He finished
eating his pizza. "I have always had the idea that one
could determine there own destiny. Even through the
limitations of space and time. I wonder what will happen
before this day is over."

~

Allen bought a copy of the newspaper with the
typical headlines on the cover. Latest murder and
robbery, some political scandal, unique yet still disturbing
news, Genetic manipulation of food, Environmental
changes he flipped through section after section of the
newspaper. The only good news was the sports section
Only one headline caught his attention; an unclaimed
winning lottery ticket in Chicago.

"Wonder what's taking them so long," he thought
turning his attention to his itinerary. He stood in line
waiting to leave St. Louis.

"Twenty one years old, and my first flight…" He
shook his head.

He began to think about the night before. Allen
took a moment to replay the events only a few hours past.

*

He had gone club hopping with his Uncle Craig
the night before. They stayed out late and did not leave
the club until after the sun came up. He rode around the
city reminiscing on places he use to hang out at. He
didn't show it but he had mixed emotions on leaving the
city. 'This is the only place I have known. It's time for me
to see something else.'

The Life and Times of Allen Court

Allen had ended up in the north side of St. Louis. He pointed his uncle's Blue Impala East, to Illinois.

A dream he had the night before had left him unnerved. His child hood friend Cynthia had been on his mind. They kept a long distance friendship going even after she left for Chicago.

'Here I am now, looking at where I will be. Like, I've seen it all before.'

"There was something about that dream it had Cynthia in it but I haven't quite been able to put them together... we were kids reading from this book... forget it, maybe it will come to me later." He arrived over his Uncles house picking up his bags. His cousin picked him up to take him to the airport.

Allen explained to him how he ended up in Finland.

"Seemed like you were doing good in college, What happened?"

"I still am. I'm just studying overseas."

"What made you pick that place?"

"My first choice was Brazil. But for school, all the classes were only in Portuguese. Then it was Costa Rica, but that was a year waiting list. By the time my school had found something that would justify me leaving, I had decided that no matter what country, it's going to have new people and a different environment to learn from."

"Pull in there I want to get something before we cross that water."

He walked in and bought two small bottles of gin to take with him on the plane.

"Hey, Hey."

Allen turned around to see one of his father's old friends, Dean. Allen could see that the years had not been good to him.

16

"You Elders boy, ain't you? It's been a while since I seen you. Me and ya, pops use to raise hell out here. We made history. Yeah." The man reminisced for a moment before speaking again. "I heard you was a writer or something."

"No, not yet, I write a little bit but I haven't really completed anything." Allen told him.

"Go ahead, kick something. Man, quit messing around and say something," Dean interrupted, staring at him. Allen started slowly, and then gathered momentum.

"Tell my soul, time to manifest higher dreams. Discovered self, from positive and negative beginnings. In my realm, light and shadow, it all dwells. Caste immediate spells, to send my evils to forgotten graves. Pure soul among equals; so much power in the people; I'll reach every goal that I find my mind truly after. As I start a new chapter I start to read. Speak, like the essence of a Nubian child, floating along the Nile, singing, 'verily, verily, life is but a dream.' I wake up. Tune heart and mind to spit that fire. To feed the curious desire, to keep lifes pages turning, feel that fire burning?"

Dean stopped him. "I like it. That's cool. Man. I don't know if I followed all of it. But I like it. Hey, hey you got some change on you?" Dean held his hand out. Allen handed him some money before leaving the store.

He sat back in the car.

"I just got some advice from Dean."

"Oh, yeah? What did he say?"

"To sum it up, that I need to take care of business." Allen looked onto the passing streets. "He might have never realized it but I looked up to him."

"Yeah, he changed a lot from when we was younger. You know how it is. Time makes people change."

"I know. But it's hard for us to look up to the "old heads" when they out asking the youngsters for crack."

"I don't know. Everything happens for a reason."

"I've heard that so much it only leaves more questions." Allen said.

"What?"

"Nothing. I'm just thinking out loud. Turn on this exit here."

The airport was right ahead.

"Well, it going to be a while cousin." Allen reached his hand out getting one last clap to his cousin before leaving. "Be easy."

Back in the present moment, Allen looked up to see it was time to leave. "I have been preparing for the worst, but I'll keep hoping for the best." He said aloud.

The flight attendant waved the passengers aboard.

~

He took a seat near the window of the plane. The next sight made him wake up.

"Maleek!" Allen smiled.   He stared in amazement at Cynthia's grandfather as he approached the seat.

"How are you, Allen?"

"I'm good, a little nervous about this flight. How come you are here?" Allen rushed out his sentences excited.

"I have just bought some land here in St. Louis that I am intending to build on." Maleek told him.

"It's been a long time since I saw you last. I think it was at my graduation?" Allen reminisced. Yeah, the last time I seen you and Cynthia together." Allen told him.

"Yes. It has been about three years. So where are you going?"

"I'm going to this country in Scandinavia, Finland."

"I have heard of the place, but I'm not truly familiar with it." Maleek said.

"Same for me." Allen said. "I've always wanted to travel, and it's working out with my school. I can go there for a few months and be home." Maleek nodded.

"When it comes to traveling, sometimes it's good just to go. Just to see different things happening in the world. I traveled to many places when I was young man. I remember seeing Miles Davis and John Coltrane performing in the sixties in Europe."

"I didn't know that you had traveled so much."

"My old Army days," Maleek paused to laugh. For a moment a smile grew across his face. This look had become more apparent to Allen over time. It was a look of one remembering the past fondly, and for one moment moving to another state of time. "I've traveled a lot. I believe that's the part Cynthia gets from me. You know she's studying at the American University of Cairo now." Maleek recognized.

"She wrote me while she was in Chicago. She told me she would be going there. I didn't get a chance to write her back."

"You never returned the message?"

"I got her information…" Allen paused for a moment. "I had planned on getting in touch with her. But you know?" Allen stopped talking. "That's life, it didn't work out." he thought privately.

The plane began roll away from the airport hanger. The plane paused briefly before taking off into the air.

"Maybe you should see her. I know she would like that." Maleek told him as the plane left the ground.

19

"I'll be closer to the North Pole, not the Burning Sands of Kemet." Allen joked.

"Cynthia would still like to see you. Besides, it would be a good experience to see where all of our history comes from."

"Maybe." Allen looked out the window at the passing ground below.

"Is there something bothering you?" Maleek asked.

"I had been thinking about a friend of mine earlier today. He passed away in an accident."

"I'm sorry to hear that." Maleek told him. Allen nodded his head slowly.

"I try to make some sense out of it, but… it changed a lot of things for me."

"I understand. Sometimes these events take us to where we need to be in life. They show us who we are. Here." Maleek pointed to his chest.

"I'm not following you, man." Allen told him.

"There was a time when our ancient ancestors, had their own visions. All people had a way of doing things that was good for them. Today, man has lost his vision and must search for his personal insight. His own kingdom if you should call it so. Kemeten people called it Ma'at. The Native American people called it the Path of the Heart. Many people call life different things but in the end you must choose how you are going to live your life."

He paused for a minute as the plane began to descend.

Maleek took some paper and wrote down a phone number.

"You know I have traveled many places and seen a lot; yet and still, many things did and did not happen for me. Not in the way I intended it at least."

"It may be the same for you. To deal with this life realistically, you must be prepared for that. Your choices will determine your life. Some of them may lead you to quit or just give up."

He passed the number to Allen.

"You can consider it fate, you can say its chance, but it will concern something you did and did not do. When you stumble along, always remember you will find your way back. Just walk with the same confidence and wisdom you have and you'll be all right." Allen nodded along letting him know he heard him. "Remember those books that you had? The one I gave your uncle but I see ended up in your hands."

"Yeah, I remember that encyclopedia set. I read the one through six editions, Cynthia read seven through twelve. We would borrow each others books. They taught me a lot about history but it was through our discussions that I learned the value of interpretation. I learned to scratch beneath the surface at times to form a clearer picture. Some of my favorite stories were in those books you gave me."

"You remember the story about life and death." Maleek asked.

"A little bit. But I'm not sure what it has to do with my situation."

"Don't think of it literally, just figuratively."

"I'll try." Allen shook his head.

Maleek pointed to the slip of paper he had wrote on.

"Give her a call sometime." Allen looked to see Cynthia's name. "She told me about the saying you two had."

"Whether, it's today or tomorrow." Allen told him.

'What's with him?' Allen contemplated. 'He goes from the 'paths, life, and death? And please, god, please don't let him bring up love. ' Allen thought.

"Cynthia still misses you." Maleek told him.

"It's not that I'm against what you say, old man." Allen thought to himself. "It's just that now, I don't want to believe in it."

The plane landed.

*

Allen sat on his second flight, from Chicago to Poland. He bought a few hip-hop CD's at Chicago O'Hare. He turned on the headphones. His mind drifted as he thought of the rest of Maleeks' conversation on the last flight.

"My granddaughter speaks a lot about you. She tells me that you have a lot of girlfriends? Been busy getting busy?"

Allen had laughed. Usually he would be proud to boast of how many women he had, but telling Cynthia's grandfather was a different story.

"Yeah, but I know how to be still and get things done, no matter if it's physical or mental," Allen stated before continuing. "But all in all, it comes down to spirit."

"I'm glad that you said that. It seems that most young men don't know that these days or if they do, they use their power in an undisciplined way."

"I cannot say I'm the most disciplined person, but I'm willing to try to be better than I have been. I just need to find my own space."

"So much of it comes down to choice." Maleek had told him. Allen meditated on it. Maleek spoke. "Do you know the last thing I remember your grandfather saying to me, about you, while he was alive?" Allen shook his head. "You are a strong man."

The moment he remembered the flight attendant strolled by.

"Would you like something to drink?"

Allen pulled the headphones off his ears.

"How much is it?" He asked.

"Complimentary."

"Okay, let me get something strong." He looked over the cart. "Give me some Cognac and a small bottle of wine."

The flight attendant obliged. Within minutes a buzz took a hold of him. He looked at the video monitor to determine the pattern airplane had taken over North America. The plane was flying over Eastern Canada.

Music began to play over the loud speakers. People were relaxed and talked all around him. He waited to get another drink before getting up to use the bathroom. By the time he returned, the dinner carts were ready. The woman handed him a cold, black tray with a small piece of fish on it.

"Excuse me, but what is this?" Allen asked.

"Smoked salmon."

"Is it cooked?"

"Yes." The flight attendant said without blinking. He cut a little piece to taste. The part he ate was stuck in his throat. He tried washing it down with the little bottle of red wine. It stayed lodged in his throat like an invisible thread.

"Let me get some sleep," he thought. "Another eleven hours on this flight," The plan rocked back and forth. "This plane moved like some type of ship, I can't imagine how the-Atlantic slave trade was." His last thought before drifting asleep.

~

The Life and Times of Allen Court

He opened his eyes from a bump in the night. He was surrounded by a huddled mass of people, stone-faced, waiting for the light of day. A fusion of night and day; he watched the sun through wood cracks. He felt pained with hunger, but did not want to eat. Neither wanting to give up or carry on, in the distance, he heard a sound. Very low like a deep chant, he remembered a past lifetime in a moments glance. "I don't like this second crossing of the Atlantic," he thought, nearly waking himself up. Rocked in a half-asleep, half-awake dream state; voices of a lost collective unconscious called to him. His body felt an eerie presence of black captives underneath the waves. "They are still calling from the sea." This was the last thought Allen had before waking up from the nightmare.

*

Allen shifted out of his seat. "What was that?" He thought, "an old memory of the triangular slave trade. That nightmare is over!"

He tried to determine how long he had been asleep. He looked at the video screen it showed the plane to be flying directly over the middle of the Atlantic Ocean.

Allen rushed to the bathroom. Feeling woozy, he felt his forehead as he stumbled in the direction of the bathroom. Blue tones from the cabin interior light washed over the other sleeping passengers faces.

Allen continued walking down the cabin. He could barely stand. A flight attendant walked by. She spoke to him in Polish, then in English. She motioned to the bathroom where he coughed up his dinner. "I'm not eating another thing on this flight."

The flight ended a few hours later. He touched down in Poland. The captain made the announcement in Polish first then in English. Allen was glad this second flight was over. "Only one more," he thought. He had a four-hour layover in the city. Allen waited in the airport hanger for his next flight.

He began to think about Cynthia. It was close to two years since he had last seen her. The last time they talked, she was telling him about the scholarship that she had received to go to school overseas. Her parents had moved north to Chicago, after her high school graduation. Initially, they had stayed in touch; calling each other often, even meeting up, every few months.

They had a relationship that had grown over the years since the first day they had met. Cynthia at times showed an interest in more than friendship, yet Allen didn't want to risk losing her as a friend.

Allen's flight number was being called. He left the station.

~

Allen finally arrived to the city of Helsinki. His ears pounded from the constant adjustment of increasing and decreasing air pressure. "Didn't know it would be this painful to fly," he thought.

Initially he was to take a bus for the last four-hour trip to Jyvaskyla. He found it to be faster to take one more flight. While waiting in Helsinki, he called his student counselor telling her to meet him outside the airport in Jyvaskyla. Allen now sat outside the small airport hanger; a thin-red haired woman pulled up in a black Saab cab.

"Are you Allen Court," the girl asked?
"Yes, I am," He answered.

25

The Life and Times of Allen Court

"I'm Myastinna and I'm here to welcome you to your new university."

He loaded all his bags into the car. They drove along making small talk. Allen looked at the modern subdivision homes that surrounded him.

"Doesn't look too much different from anything in middle-class America," he thought.

Myastinna pointed out other student buildings before taking him to his university dorm room in the Kortehlia housing building.

"I hope you enjoy yourself here," She told him before leaving.

"I'll try." He carried his luggage to his room. Going downstairs to grab his last bag, he ran into a group of students walking out to go to a night club.

One of them asked if he would like to join them.

Allen first told him "no," due to his exhaustion from being in the air so long. On further thought, he knew it would be a good way to become acquainted to some of the other exchange students. He walked back downstairs and was greeted by a group of students living in his apartment complex. Another student introduced himself to Allen.

"Hello, I'm Julien." The blond haired French man said to him, extending his hand to Allen.

Julien introduced two other French students to him Mari and Jean. "These two here are from Germany," pointing to a six foot-five giant named Mark and a short brunette named Emily. Julien finished the introduction pointing to two Italians, one named Fernando and a girl named Natalia.

"I'm Allen. Why are you all waiting right here to go to the club?"

"We're waiting for our cabs to arrive," Emily said. No sooner than she mentioned it, two white Mercedes and a black Mercedes sedan pulled up to pick up their passengers.

"These are the taxis around here?" Allen asked, Raul, a Portuguese man, nodded his head yes.

"I wonder what else is good here." He thought, cramming himself in the back of the new Mercedes. The car sped through empty streets taking only a few minutes to get into the center of town.

Once outside the club, Allen waited thirty minutes before entering. He walked in after paying the cashier in Finn marks, the countries currency. He could hear loud techno music. He wanted to leave.

"I got to get out of here." Allen told Ben, a Canadian exchange student.

"Why," Ben asked?

"This music is too much, plus my head is ringing. I knew there wouldn't be a lot of my type of music here; but I was thinking that there would be at least a little hip-hop somewhere around here."

"Actually there is." Ben explained. "There's a place called Bounce where you can go to and hear hip-hop, but only on Wednesdays. You will have to wait a week, since its Thursday." Ben told him. But wait, there is another club called Blaze and you can go there anynight."

"I'm about to leave now. I see some other students have started to go." Allen left the building heading towards the taxi carport. He started a conversation with a young Italian girl named Raffia. He tried to tell her his name was Allen but the closest she had come to was Ali. Finally, after three minutes Raffia, boldly told Allen that he "could not speak good English!"

"Good." Allen replied. "You'll be one less person I got to talk too, ya dig. I mean…. understand." Allen told her as the cab approached. Within minutes, he was back at the apartment complex. "I need to get some rest," he thought, falling asleep.

Chapter 2
Beautiful Things

Allen woke from a hazy dream. He raised himself from the bed looking for his backpack, grabbing a piece of paper from his notebook. Writing the first things that came to his mind, Allen repeated the words trying to capture the emotions of the moment, before he lost it.

"Peace," he repeated aloud. He began writing in his notepad. "I can't find it here. Man, what was Maleek talking about? The Life and Death story; what was that about?" Allen re-told the story writing it along in his notebook. "It was about two brothers." He began to remember.

"One was named Life, the other named Death." What's next? "Life had been given a gift and it was placed within a beautiful box. Everyday life would look at the box. All the while, Death was around the corner watching; waiting for his chance to steal what Life had. One day when life had taken his eye off the gift, Death took the box. Life returned to find that his gift was gone. He cried out to his father, "Death, stole my prize." His father sat calmly as Life complained. "My son," his father said, "All the while Death has been watching you, I had been watching Death. While you slept, I took the prize. All Death holds is an empty box. I still have the gift.'"

"What is the gift?" Allen dropped the pen on the desk. "It didn't mean much the first time I read it; something's different now." Trying to relax, he lay awake, yearning for sleep. The deafening ring in his ear,

kept him awake. He contemplated the twenty hours
flight time and delays and figured it to be four a.m. in
Finnish time.

"What does that make it back home? Eleven p.m.
No wonder I can't sleep. I haven't had any rest in two
days." His body felt tired. He closed his eyes, feigning
for rest. Soon as he felt himself coming close to losing
consciousness, a random thought would pull him from
his slumber. He lightly ran his fingers through his hair,
one thought breaking into the next.

"And next week I can get my hair...wait a minute.
Next week? There is no next week that I am used to. I
won't be home until... When I will be home?" Instantly,
Allen felt unbearably alone. "I've got to find my way on
my own." He stared at the bare walls, feeling as if they
were pressing along his chest. "I need to get a television
it's just too quiet here. I need some sound, some noise,
something. My music, that's' it! I will buy a stereo first
thing tomorrow. This silence is too much."

~

Allen awoke hearing a noise from outside the
building. Looking down from his second story window;
there was a group of students below. He put on some
clothes and left the room.

"Time to meet the neighbors;" he thought. Allen
walked out. He recognized the German man, Mark and
two Italian girls Raffia and Natalia from the night before.

"What happened with you?" Mark asked.

"I had to get some rest." Allen replied.

Emily walked up saying "hello." A short man,
stood next to him.

"Who are you?"

"Daniel, and you?"

"I'm Allen. Where are you from?"

"Barcelona, Espana."

"Spain?" Allen asked. The man nodded. "I'm from the US."

"That is very good," Daniel said nodding enthusiastically. "I want to improve my English. It's good to find a natural speaker."

"I want to improve my Spanish; we can trade phrases. Maybe you can tell me about the Moorish influence still there. A look. I'm about to walk into the city. If you like, we can walk together." Allen noticed Daniel had a black sweater on. "Ain't you hot?"

Daniel shook his head no, then yes.

"Hace, muy caliente."

"I say you're crazy, for wearing that hot sweater."

Daniel nodded. "He might be all right," Allen thought. Allen turned back to Emily.

"What are you about to do?" He asked her.

"We are about to go to the supermarket. It's right down this street." Emily pointed westward. "You want to come along?"

"No, but thank you; I'm going into town just to see how things look around here." Allen motioned in the opposite direction, east.

"We'll see you later. The group you met, yesterday, is going to get together later tonight to eat. Fernando is cooking tonight, osso bocco or cabinara, some Italian dish." Emily said, unsure of which one.

"You're welcome to eat with us." She added. Mark nodded yes.

"I live on the second floor of Kortehlia." Mark told him. We're all meeting up at my apartment at about eight."

"I might. You're right down the hall from me. I guess I'll be seeing you around. Later." Allen told them as they started for the grocery store. He turned around to see that Daniel had not moved.

"Come on then, let's see what we can get into. We have about a week before classes actually start. We may as well get used to the city." They walked to an electronics' store and talked with a cashier.

Allen paid for a stereo receiver and speakers but would return to pick it up later.

"My mission is done for today. You want to go back?" Daniel nodded yes.

"All right; but now, since we know our way by foot lets, take a car back."

Daniel, short and stocky built, looked like a bull. He had just arrived to the University in the morning. Knowing how cliques form early, he decided to make a group of his own.

The two rode in the back of a Saab cab taking in the sights. Allen looked to see that gas was sold in liters instead of gallons. What stood out to him was that the liters were the same prices as gallons as the United States. That means they were paying more than double the price then he was used to. Daniel looked at a group of students. Crowds of young kids held conversations on small Nokia cellular phones. Girls wore five inch stack heeled boots as they walked in and out of the department stores.

"See anything you like?" Allen asked. Daniel nodded, pointing at one Finnish girl in a flowing, canary-yellow colored dress. A light breeze lifted the corners of her dress, exposing long slender legs. The car began to turn back towards the woods. Trees grew thick next to each other on top of the hills. The leaves varied in hues of red, orange, green; the color of changing autumn leaves. Daniel spoke out suddenly in admiration of the sights.

"Estamos, en el mundo para hacer cosas buenas." Daniel said looking out the window nodding. Allen agreed, repeating Daniels phrase in English.

"We're here to do good things in this world."
Allen repeated in English looking ahead towards the
rolling green hills that lay in front of them. "Big things
my friend; beautiful things."

Chapter 3
Future Possibilities

Allen walked into the packed bar, his hand trailed
over the gold rail that aligned the long hallway to the
dance floor. Daniel had talked him into going out with
the other students. Now he stood in the middle of a
crowded floor absorbing the energy of the people.
Most of the patrons were students from the university.
He noticed two separate groups of exchange students
starting to form their own groups. Allen had yet to
commit to any particular one, choosing to remain free.

Mixing in with a handful of people at a time, he
looked over a Spanish girl named Marina. He had spoken
with her for a few minutes finding out she was from
Madrid. Allen nudged Daniel to see what he thought of
her. Daniel looked her over and gave her a thumb down.
Allen agreed moving away from her. He walked to the
bar to order his first beer of the night. Allen stood
around the bar when a tall man walked by him. Allen had
seen him with the other exchange students. The man
looked him up and down before speaking.

"You are from the US," the man asked the
question with a slight doubt raised in his voice?

"Born and raised." Allen replied calmly. "And
you? Where are you from?"

"I'm from Austria. Do you know where that is?"
The man said in a challenging manner. Allen nodded.

"Yeah, I know where it is." He told him.

The man's face held a disbelieving smile. "You don't know where it is?" The man told him.

"It was in Austria where a small group of people assassinated an Austrian prince along a bridge, which helped to start World War I." Allen replied cynically.

"You do know where it is!" The man said surprised.

"Yeah, I do. See you later." Allen walked off into the crowd. You want me to prove something to you and I just met you. Clear sign someone I don't want you in my life. Allen thought angrily. Then he thought about it some more. "Yeah, I can recall some of my high school history lessons." Allen finished his beer, running back into Daniel.

"I'm getting a little bored here, I'm thinking about bouncing." Allen told Daniel. He turned to head for the door; before he could take another step, a new arrival caught his eye.

A tall girl with olive skin walked in wearing a long burgundy dress. "Now *that's* what I am talking about!" The girl's curly black hair bounced along her shoulders. Her gray eyes scanned the room. He looked at her long thin figure he could tell she was foreign. Allen walked up to her.

"She doesn't look Finnish, unless she's mixed." He thought, following her to the dance floor.

She was with two other women. They danced in a circle amongst each other. The girl looked bored as she moved with the music. The DJ changed the music. A west coast hip- hop song blared through the speakers.

The girls moved on approvingly. Allen moved next to the girl. In moments, they were dancing together. The girl's bored expression had shifted. She openly smiled to him. He motioned towards a table were they went to talk.

"You move like girls back home." Allen told her. "How long have you been here?"

"I've lived here for five years. I'm Iranian" The girl said slowly. "I wish I could leave but I have to finish college first."

"Sounds like a plan." Allen told her. "Look, I was just about to leave but if you give me your number, I'll call you."

The girl wrote her name and number down. "Zaleha."

"I'll call her," he thought, leaving the bar.

*

Zaleha volunteered to show Allen around the city. He accepted and gave her his address. He heard the hallway buzzer and left his bed to answer it. She walked in and was casually dressed in sweat pants and T-shirt. They left the building where a group of students standing in front of the bike racks. Raul, a Portuguese student, and the Austrian man were in awe of Zaleha as she walked by. Allen waved hello to them as they stood with their mouths wide open. He overheard the two saying 'the American' and noticed them point to him.

Zaleha brought him back to the moment and pointed to a bus stop.

"We can go to my friend's house." She said. They took the bus, riding though the orderly streets of Jyvaskyla.

"All of these houses follow the same pattern if they are on the same block; matter of fact I don't see any apartment building that stands over twelve floors high." Allen commented. "Most of these buildings have the same structure and color to them."

Zaleha pushed the stop button on the bus. They stopped in front of the mall. Throughout the day, she introduced him to a number of people. One of the most interesting of them happened to be a young Nigerian man named Raheem. Long face and stocky build, Raheem was also an exchange student. With a steel glare, noncommittal yet watchful glances, he reminded Allen of a panther.

Allen had walked with Zaleha and three of her classmates to club Bounce. While walking through the door, a familiar bass line dropped from a rap song that quickly caught Allen's attention. When he looked up, he noticed a tall, black man instructing a Finnish boy as the boy looked down at a piece of paper in his hand. The boy was rattling off words when Allen walked in. The lyrics kept switching back and forth from English verses then into a Finnish chorus. Allen calmly sat down as Raheem blatantly stared at him. His face was angrily set in stone as Zaleha slid next to Allen. The two performers finished their set and walked over to Zaleha and her girl friends.

The Finnish boy started to grab and hold onto one of the gypsy girls. He was dressed in baggy, camouflage pants and an oversized blue T-shirt with matching blue gym shoes. He turned his attention to Allen and asked him if he was a rapper. Allen shook his head no.

The performer lost interest in talking with him. Raheem walked over and started speaking to Zaleha in Finnish.

"Did they have something going?" Allen thought. Raheem turned and looked coldly at Allen.

~

Allen read through the course catalogue while he sat through the first hours of orientation. Eight other students were in the conference room. The exchange students had to introduce themselves by stating their names and the countries they were from. There was one other American in the room. Kane Richardson sat along the long table staring at the orientation instructor. At twenty-eight he was one of the older students in the room. He looked at hip-hop Allen and didn't know what to think.

"I don't want any problems so I will just keep my distance from him." Kane thought.

"My name is Kane, my major is Sports Recreational Therapy," he announced to the class.

"I wonder if he is prejudice. No matter where you go, some things stay the same. With long hair and shaggy beard, he looks as if he had taken care of a few farms." Allen thought, staring at Kane.

"Yeah, I know you expected to see some Americans; but I know you definitely didn't think you would have a brotha' over here with you. It's okay. I'm here to visit." Allen thought as he nodded towards Kane.

*

Allen was in the university counselors office reading over the courses he was going to take. He chose Chemistry, Biology, Finnish language for Beginners, and Finnish ball games. All of the classes were to be held in between late afternoon Monday and Thursday morning. If he wanted to travel he would have the time open.

After a twenty minute wait, the counselor called him into the office. When he stood up, he could see a bright smile flash from a newly arrived African girl.

"I'm going to have to check her out before the day is over," he thought. The girl had plans of her own. Before he could enter, the girl caught him in front of the doorway.

"Where are you from?" She asked.

"The US, and you?"

"I'm from here." She told him.

"Really, that's a surprise." He could hear the counselor getting restless. "Hey, hold up a minute and let me turn in my classes. I'll talk with you afterwards." The girl nodded. Allen walked into the counselors' office.

"Hei," Allen said in Finnish for hello.

"Hei," The counselor smiled earnestly.

"Mita Kullu?" Allen continued, it was the equivalent to "how are you" in English.

"Hyvaa! That's good." The woman exclaimed. "You know some Finnish already?"

"I'm going to learn as much as possible. I enrolled in the class here. Suomi for beginners. Allen in turn handed his schedule over to her. She read it over.

"I'm thinking about buying a television."

"Really?" The woman said with a curious intonation in her voice. "Why?"

"I believe it will help me get accustomed to hearing people speak the language and hearing the pronunciation. Any shows that have subtitles I will be able to listen and read the text."

"Are you enjoying yourself here?" she asked.

"I am. I like the weather; I love the sun and the long days. There's about what, eighteen hours of daylight now?" Allen told her.

"Yes, in the peak of summer, twenty. Enjoy it now because in the winter, it will be just the opposite." She reminded him before handing over his printed schedule.

"All your classes should go through fine. If you have any questions, be sure to give me a call. I know you will do well here. Oh, by the way, there will be a student cruise for the exchange students tomorrow. All the information is in this paper. I hope to see you there."

"Thank you." Allen left the room taking the paper. He stepped through the door and the smiling girl stood in front of him.

"And who might you be?" Allen asked.

"I'm Vivian, and you are?"

"Allen. Where are you living? I'm in Kortehelia. Where are you from?"

"I was born in Mali, Africa. That is where my mother lives and my father is Finnish. That is how I got here."

Vivian had her number announced over a loud speaker.

"I heard about the student cruise tomorrow. Are you going?" Allen asked.

"Yes. I'll see you there." Vivian waved goodbye walking into the counselors' office.

Allen headed for the cafeteria. He walked alone outside and stopped to ask a couple of students the best place to eat at. They happened to be two American exchange students. There respective states were Florida and Pennsylvania. One man pointed the way with a silly grin along his face. Allen could not resist asking him why he was so happy.

"We just came back from Stockholm, Sweden," Pennsylvania told him. "Whatever you do, you have to go there. "

"Why is that?" Allen asked.

"The girls look, so good," The man from Florida jumped in. "I just wish we had more time."

"I should have signed up for classes in Sweden." Pennsylvania said aloud. A man yelled ahead of them. "We got to go. But seriously, if you have the chance to go, do it. You won't be disappointed."

"I'll keep it in mind," Allen headed for the cafeteria and entered the dining hall. Eruptions of conversations were going on around him. He looked for some students he was familiar with while standing in line.

Meat and potatoes were the main course. He opted for fish, salad, potatoes and bread. The glass cups used for drinking were smaller than his hands. He was waved over by the French students. Julien talked with Mari about the classes they were taking that semester. Near Allen, was a thin Finnish man. He introduced himself as Cannci. He talked and ate.

Allen pulled back his seat to leave. He looked for the trash can and was surprised to see a long line of students waiting to place there trash in three different recycling bins. The other foreign students had eaten all the food on their plate. He looked down on his plate noticing that he had left large portions of food on his plate.

"My eyes are bigger than my stomach." Allen thought.

Scrapping off the last bit of food, Allen headed to the city. He had to return to the city to buy some CD's. While walking around the mall, he stopped at a video store. He flipped through the movie selections. A medium build, blond girl with a round bottom caught his attention. She walked near him assisting another customer.

"How are you?" Allen asked. The girls smile widened.

"I'm good. You're from the States aren't you?" The girl asked excitedly.

"Yeah, and you?"

"I'm from here, but I went to school in Arizona."

"Arizona?" Allen asked, "How was that?"

"It was fun. I didn't get to go out much, but I liked it. I kind of miss how friendly people are there. My name is Saga by the way."

"I'm Allen."

"You are living in the student complex right?"

"Yeah, I am."

"Maybe we can hang out sometime."

"It's all good. Give me your number. I'll call you. I need someone to show me around." The girl turned toward her register and wrote down her telephone number. Allen looked her over as she turned around. "She has a nice body and a cute face with pretty gray eyes. Today has been a good day," he thought. He gave her his number as well. "I'll call her during the week," he thought heading for the electronic store he had visited with Daniel.

He walked into the store. A tall black woman caught his attention. Allen looked and could feel the anger in her eyes.

"Should I talk to her?" He contemplated looking her over. "She would be the second black girl I met since coming here. It will be good to have one school chick and one local girl. She is kind of wild looking; but what can I expect, it's Finland." The girl continued to stare as he approached.

"What up, how are you?" Allen asked her. The girl smiled, lowering her guard for a moment.

"Why did you come here?" She asked, Allen could hear the scorn in her voice.

"I'm an exchange student. It's not a permanent move, just for school. Were you born here?"

"No, I was born in Uganda. My mother is Finnish my father is from Uganda. We came here with my father when I was thirteen."

"Oh, so you speak Finnish well then?"

"I understand it, but I refuse to speak it."

"Why do you refuse to speak?"

"When I first arrived as a child, people were not use to foreigners, especially blacks. I had a hard time in

40

school, being teased by Finnish kids and fighting everyday."

The girl lifted her hand through her coarse curly hair exposing a ring.

"So you married, huh?" Allen noticed.

"Engaged." She chuckled "He's Finnish. But... I have a sister if you are looking for someone," she added.

"That's something." Allen paused. "You offer me your sister before you give me your name?" The girl smirked. "I'm Allen. Soon to be your brother-in-law if your sister works nearly as fast as you." The smirk turned into a smile as she caught on.

"Tarena."

Allen turned his attention from her for a moment surveying the new televisions and not finding any matching his price range.

"I don't see any TV's here that I want, so I'm about to go. Tomorrow my school is having a cruise around Jyvaskyla Lake. I've never been on a boat before but I think it should be fun. Do you want to come?" The girl smiled

"I would love to, Brother."

Chapter 4
Fair Weather Friends

The clouds were heavy in the sky. Allen arrived early at the boat dock, taking a seat upon a bench looking at the calm waters. Saga had surprised him and gave him a call the same day. After speaking with her, he could tell she had the mix, of intelligence and cleverness he liked. Allen invited her over to visit within the week. "I haven't decided what I am going to do with her, but she seems like a cool girl." While thinking about Saga, Tarena approached.

"How are you, brother?"

"I'm good. I wonder how this boat ride is gonna be."

"Usually they're fun. People basically drink until they get fall over drunk." Tarena told him.

"It ain't that serious for me." Allen replied.

"Oh, Yeah." Tarena looked at him skeptically. "We'll see later. I'm going to give you this drink called salmolak."

"That's black licorice right?" Allen asked.

Tarena nodded her head. "And I'm going to buy you two shots."

The students from the university began crowding around the boat dock. A burly Finnish man waved to the students to board the ship. Allen walked on with Tarena following behind him. The boat rocked as the people came on board.

Allen walked to the hull of the ship taking a look around. He climbed a stairwell to find the bar. He took a seat by the window as the boat pulled away from the harbor. Tarena sat beside him as Allen looked around at the new students coming in the room.

Allen later walked out on the deck and watched the water roll over itself creating white foam bubbles as the boat picked up speed. He overheard a woman behind speaking English with an American accent. He turned to see a chubby, light-skinned, black girl talking with a Finnish couple about African-American sororities.

"And if you don't do that, they won't consider you 'made', the foreign couple had confused looks on their faces but nodded in politeness before walking off.

"They don't know what she's talking about," Allen thought. Allen waited for the couple to leave as the girl leaned over the rail alone.

"What's up? I can tell you are from back home." He said.

The girl smiled brightly, her green eyes shined. "Cute face," Allen thought.

"Hi. My name is Niki," she told him.

"How long have you been here?" Allen asked her.

"About two weeks. I haven't been doing much. This is the first time I really had a chance to go out." Allen nodded as she talked.

"I know you get this question a lot, but what made you come here?" he asked.

"I wanted to experience what going to school in another country would be like. See the world before I decided on any future career moves. And you?"

"The same thing; I wanted to do this before settling down." Allen told her.

While they talked, the girl from the guidance counselors office, Vivian, walked over. Allen turned and introduced them. They spoke to each other as if they were the best of friends. Allen began to think of Tarena.

"I invited this girl from town here. Come with me so I can introduce you to her." They agreed and followed Allen back down into the cabins. They found the bar where Tarena was looking out the window onto the rolling waves. Allen approached her and she gave him a nod. He immediately introduced the two girls to her.

"Tarena, this is Niki and Vivian. They go to school with me." The girls mingled happily with one another as they began ordering drinks.

Tarena ordered a shot of Salmolak for him. It looked like watered down tar. Allen hesitantly put his hand around the shot glass.

The Life and Times of Allen Court

"I don't know if I'm going to like this?" Allen raised the floating shot glass to his face. The smell hit his nostrils, causing him to rock back. Just as he was about to toss down the drink, Vivian took a hold of his arm.

"Is this the first time you ever had this?" She asked.

"Yes."

The three girls laughed together, intertwined in some private joke.

"Wait, I want to get a picture of this." Vivian pulled a silver camera from her purse. "Okay, drink."

He turned the black liquor up and almost spit the few drops of the bitter drink out. The women laughed as his face balled up at the drink.

"That is the nastiest drink I've ever tasted."

"We like it," the girls said happily. They continued ordering drinks.

"I'm hanging out with some lushes." Allen said looking around. "I'm going to walk around for a minute, I'll be back." He told them.

He talked briefly with a girl from France while watching the end of a poetry performance in the downstairs compartment of the boat. Some people tried their hand at karaoke. The boat ride was coming to an end.

~

"I want to hook Allen up with my sister Melinda." Tarena had thought while she was on the boat. "But this new girl, Vivian, is going to get in the way. Vivian told me that she likes Allen. What can I say to make her change her mind about him?" Tarena thought craftily. "Maybe, I can tell her that he asked my sister to go on a date with him."

Tarena waited for Vivian to walk into the bathroom. She walked in quietly behind her. Vivian looked at herself in the mirror. Tarena washed her hands slowly under the water before speaking with Vivian.

"What do you think of Allen?"

"I don't know, he seems nice so far." Vivian looked at Tarena. "Well, you know there aren't a lot of nice looking black guys around. He seems down to earth."

"Don't let him fool you. He is just another player."

"Really?" Vivian asked.

"You know he is trying to date my sister." Tarena told Vivian sowing the seeds of doubt in her mind.

"What?" She answered suspiciously.

"When I first met him, he asked if I had a sister," continued Tarena. "He wanted to take her out. I just thought you should know."

"I can't believe the nerve of that guy!" Vivian said loosing her composure. "And I liked him, too! Well I'm going to have to give him a piece of my mind. Later tonight! I know what we can do." Vivian said, falling into Tarena's trap. The boat docked. Allen returned from the karaoke session.

"Ready to go?" Vivian asked. Allen nodded. They found a cab a few minutes after leaving the boat. Before returning to Kortehelia they took a slight divergence. Tarena whispered to Allen that they wanted to go to a strip club. Allen being a perfect gentleman, obliged.

They walked into the strip club. A dancer gyrated, long and strong over the center stage. Four women were dancing along circular stages around her.

Vivian began to turn her desire upon Allen, rubbing her hands down his chest.

"We can continue this later." She gave him a kiss around the neck.

45

"We might be able to do that." He nodded to the girls. "It's time to go"

*

Tarena had decided to go home but Vivian told Allen that she was going to sleep over at Niki's apartment. They arrived back to the apartment complex. The girls left the cab giggling. Allen said his goodbyes, glad to be returning to his bed. He had not wanted to rush into anything with Vivian, preferring to let time play things out. He was surprised at how she came on to him in the club.

"I still haven't gotten her number yet, but maybe the next time I see her I can get it." His phone rang. Allen turned to look at his clock seeing the time flashed three a.m., "Who is this?" He thought walking to the phone. Maybe some family he thought lifting the receiver.

"What's up?"

"Hi, it's Vivian." Allen face broke into a smile.

"I was wondering if I can come down to tell you something."

"It must be important, it's so late. Yeah, come down."

"I'll see you in a minute."

Allen hung up the phone with a shake of his head.

"My first booty call at three in the morning." He heard the hall door buzzer. He let her in as she walked swiftly through his hall door. Her hips swayed as she stepped into his bedroom. She stood for a moment looking at the layout of his room; standing before the open window.

"I see you have a big bed."

"I need room." He walked over to his bed sitting down. "How did you get my number?"

"I looked you up on the printout with all the other foreign students' phone numbers." Vivian continued looking out the window into the dark.

"Cute and resourceful. I knew there was something about you I liked. So, what do you want?" He asked, not assuming he knew why she had come.

"I have something to tell you." He patted the side of his bed, she sat beside him.

"I don't know if I should say this now?"

"Oh, yeah?" Allen's arm slid around her.

"I don't know if I should say this now?" She repeated, pausing for a moment. "Or, if I should wait until I hate you more?"

"Hate me, more?" Allen questioned. His hand rose to the middle of her back; their eyes coming together.

"I think you are a lowdown, conniving, snake."

"Really?" Allen leaned in with Vivian meeting him in for a kiss. She lifted her hand to his chest then wrapped around them around his back. Allen could feel the heat in him rise up, but did not push. They stopped. Vivian suddenly stood up, straitening out her clothes, regaining her composure.

"I just wanted to say that."

"It's been said but, why did you say it?" He said nonchalantly, Vivian gave him a sharp look.

"You are trying to get me and Tarena sister at the same time?"

"No. Not for real. Tarena told me she has a sister, that's all." Allen looked at her. "Is that it? You think I was trying to get you two?"

"Well, why would she say that?" Vivian asked.

"I don't know," he said aloud. "So they were setting me up the whole time. I gotta cancel this," he thought.

47

"Look, it's too late for all the he said she said. You two girls working together is bad business. Don't believe all that you hear." Allen told her.

"Well, why…" Vivian continued.

"I don't know why, I just need some rest." Allen told her. "Take care of yourself."

"I'll call you tomorrow? In the morning if it's okay?" She asked.

"Anytime, you are always welcome." She walked out the door, with no more words.

Chapter 5
Trust

A week had gone by and Allen made it a point to make himself known to the microscopic foreign population. Within days, the back of his notebook was filled with the names of exchange students and African immigrants. He was slowly becoming acquainted with his new home. He had been with Zaleha, walking through the mall, when she ran onto a group of her friends. Raheem had approached the group as Allen listened to music over his headphones. Raheem started talking about music with Allen offering to let Raheem to listen to some of his CD's. He had agreed to meet Raheem later in the week in the at the student bar.

Allen asked him where did black people go to get their haircut. Raheem's had been complaining that the style of clippers in Finland were not sharp enough to get close skin fades.

"You got those clippers that can get me those close fades? The clippers they have here, is for straight thin hair. I can't use razors; they make my skin break out."

"I got some liners for you. They'll hook it up." Allen replied. "I was thinking it wouldn't be any, so I brought my own."

"No. No." Raheem countered defensively. "We do have those type, you just have go to Helsinki to get them."

"Give me a call later; I'll hook it up for free."

A few days later, Raheem had taken Allen up on the offer. It took nearly an hour to cut his hair. He kept twisting in the chair while Allen jumped back and forth between two sets of clippers and his battery operated groomsman. Raheem had brought over an extra set of clippers and a small mirror. He kept checking Allen's work, constantly holding up the mirror commenting on the way he was working.

"This cat's vain." Allen thought, as he went over the pencil-thin goatee Raheem wore. After a ten-minute hair lining, he was finally satisfied. Two days later, Allen had three paying African customers as well as one Finnish student.

Raheem came to meet Allen at the student recreation center a few days afterwards. Allen liked talking to Raheem. He did not have any pretensions of superiority over Allen simply because he was from Africa. Raheem was a straight talker, and told him how it was from the get. He even pulled him aside to tell him a few things.

"As long as you have dough, you're cool, but if not, you're stuck. You may as well take your ass home and come back when you get it!"

"Seems like, that's life all over the world." Allen told him.

"It's the world we live in. But man, you're cool over here. You got a fat chain," Raheem pointed to Allen's necklace "and the latest clothes. You'll make out fine, especially with Zaleha."

"What? That's it?" Allen asked.

"You will find out soon enough." Raheem finished.

Allen laughed. "Yeah; okay. I ain't dumb I know some of these European girls only like me for the novelty affect. Let me try that; but then when they talk with me they find a real person."

Raheem nodded.

"What's going on in Nigeria? Did you grow up there?" Allen asked Raheem.

"I was born there, but my father moved me here right afterwards. I'm from the Yoruba tribe. Since I have dual citizenship, I'd go back every few years but I don't stay too long. I ended up going to high school for a year in Nigeria." A waiter came over with two beers.

"When I first got there, I was "dumb." But, then… I got smart."

"What you mean "got smart?"" Allen asked.

"Cats was outsmarting me with my own money. They would be like, "let me come in." I'd open my door to my crib, and they was stealing my shit on the sly; all that. I grew up around here, you know. Here, you don't have to worry about people trying to rob you. Everybody got money or get it from the government. But man, in Nigeria, they'll kill you over pennies." He said seriously.

Allen turned around as a skinny blond brought over the thin crust cheese pizza. The food took a lot of getting use to as Allen cut into the center of the pizza. In every pizza parlor, customers would order pizzas with the most absurd toppings. He would hear orders of, blue cheese and anchovies and so forth. After watching two hungry school kids eating eggs baked on top a soggy pizza, he had to turn around from the restaurant.

Mentality wise, Raheem and Allen were enough alike to share the same table.

"And then, those dudes were trying to give me the game." Raheem started again. "At first, they were giving me the knowledge; then when I started baggin' chicks they couldn't get, they was like, 'how you do that?'" Allen laughed.

"I know what you mean." Allen laughed with him.

"Yeah, by the end of that year, the same people who had put me down on game... was coming to me for answers."

"If that's the case, what's up with Zaleha. You know she's fine but..." Allen shook his head... I don't know."

"Zaleha, she looks good but...she's dumb." Allen started laughing.

"Why you say that?"

"It's just her way. You'll see," he continued further, "It may be because she came here so late. A lot of people have a hard time adjusting when they move here as teenagers. It's cool though. You don't have to worry about being homeless or nothing like the States. Here it's easy. There's' a lot of good people here once you get to know them. Education is free. But the more money you make; the more in taxes you pay to keep everything even. The government will hit you up on taxes. Some people are paying forty and sixty percent. That's why I want to go to the States." He paused smiling. "There, you can blow up."

"Maybe so, but don't go thinking life is gravy. You hardly ever think about Native Americans on reservations. You don't hear people talking about a prison system with no real rehabilitation. And people

51

ain't saying a thing about how drugs changed everything. Don't believe, "it's all good," like those movies you watch. Something called Manifest Destiny was the creed and look what it did, it manifested an entire new reality."

"What?" Raheem asked.

"What I am saying is that there still is racism going on but for some people; mainly white people, it's not relative to them."

"What?" Raheem asked again as Allen continued.

"People tend to look at life and turn things around in accordance to what *they* want to believe. For example, if you ask ten white people what is the biggest problem facing America, more than likely you will get nearly ten different answers. You will hear answers like war, taxes, terrorism, the environment; maybe, one will say, racism. Turn the same question around and ask ten black people and eight out of ten, will say racism. The difference in answers, show the division of thought."

"It seems like people are doing well over there." Raheem retorted.

"Don't get it wrong. You can get whatever you want in life. Here or there, when it comes to material. But it's not going to be easy. You're going to have put in something; time, money, effort, patience, is all needed to attain your goals."

"So that's it?" Raheem laughed at him. "What's the world to you?"

"I don't know yet. I'm still putting that together. What I do know is I'm gonna get what I need but all the extra; I'm gonna have to earn that." Allen told him.

"I was looking through your CD case; you got some music I haven't heard of."

"I keep different styles. What's messed up, is that the kids who like hip-hop hardly can't always get the new music because it doesn't get the money for airplay. I got some underground hip-hop, some commercial stuff you might know, and some other off the hinges, banging hits. I'll let you hold some of it."

Raheem raised his eyebrows. Allen explained. "I figure people over here can only get to listen to a small portion of the music that is coming from the US."

"I got some East and West coast joints." Raheem told him.

"I got that and more. I believe, pretty soon, you are going to be hearing a lot of music from the South, even the Midwest. You have all these different states putting out music. Like how its separate countries here, but it's all one at home." Raheem nodded understanding.

"I have this one CD. I can't loan that one out because I listen to it every single day." He said with a grin. "Go out and buy it, then you'll understand."

"What's up with your boy Cancci?" Allen asked.

"He's real chill." Raheem answered. "You can trust him with anything. He's one of the smartest people I know. He speaks five languages, fluently." He paused.

"He's half, Finnish, half, Spanish." Raheem told him.

"You know, when I talked with him, he told me that he is going to be a diplomat."

"He'll make it." Raheem said seriously.

"I don't doubt it. He carries himself like a diplomat already. It's just that, where I'm from… I don't hear many people aiming for things like that. With the way I can be, I may have to ask him for amnesty in the future."

Raheem chuckled, catching Allen's joke. "Cool." Allen thought, "someone I can relate to over here." The waitress came over placing the check on the table.

Raheem put his hand inside his pocket. "Hey, I left my wallet in my bag. Give me your keys, so I can get it. It's in your room."

"Don't worry about the check, I'll get it. If you want, you can pay me back later, when we return." Allen told him.

"You don't have to go back. I'll go and get it." Raheem insisted.

"That's all right." Allen said firmly.

"What? You don't trust me?" He asked waiting for Allen's response. Allen did not want to say no; but after hearing Raheem's stories of his previous naiveté to foreign flim flams, Allen preferred to learn from others previous mistakes.

"We'll go together."

*

"I should call Cynthia now," Allen thought as he waited in his room. Before he could dial, the phone rang. It was Saga. She wanted to come over and visit him. He told her to come. Allen thought of the possible relationships he could have. After the Vivian incident, he decided to take his time on love connections. Vivian was looking like a good prospect, but she was unsure of herself, being easily misled by Tarena. Saga knew what she wanted, making it easier for her to obtain it. "If I have to choose so far, I would say Saga has the advantage." He heard his doorbell ring. Saga came inside, greeting Allen with a kiss.

"I see you are not shy." Allen pulled back.

"I don't think I should be." She told him still holding on.

"Aren't you worried that I may have other girls?"

"I can't stop that from happening, the only thing I can deal with is the time I have now." She spoke firmly and with enough conviction to impress Allen. They kissed again but now in a more passionate way. Speaking on many things Allen began to voice his concerns to Saga.

"I miss home." Allen confessed.

"I was sure that you would be about now. Saga told him.

"Well one good thing is that I will not be gone forever, just a few months."

"One thing that I miss about the U.S. is the food." Saga said. "Over there, you get huge amounts of food when you order and it's so cheap."

"The food tastes different here. All of the juices taste like lightly flavored water." Allen said.

"We don't have as much sugar in our drinks as you guys do."

"Well, if you ask me it all tastes better at home." Allen looked at the clock seeing it was passed nine. "You should be going home about now." Saga looked at the time and agreed.

"Will I see you tomorrow?" She asked.

"If you call?" Allen told her.

She did.

Chapter 6
New Arrival

Allen's first days of classes went by quickly. Allen's science courses were little more than reviews of past classes. One class that stood out was his Finnish ball games class.

His Suomi for Beginners class had become increasingly more difficult. Allen spent hours after school reading, learning a new vocabulary and various pronunciations. Going out in his spare time, he met even more students. One student in particular, Steffan, a reserved history major from Belgium, had organized a one day trip to Stockholm for the exchange students. Steffan, asked Allen if he wanted to take go along for the cruise.

"How much will it cost?" Allen asked.

"If we can get fifteen people to come, it will be very cheap. About twenty dollars per person." Steffan scratched his horn rimmed glasses. "All you would need to do is pay for the train ride to Turku."

"When are we going?"

"We are leaving tomorrow, Thursday. So if you want to go you have to pay me today." Steffan told him, Allen reached into his pocket and paid him in Finn Marks.

"Okay, now." Steffan said. "You should be at the train station at around four o'clock tomorrow."

~

Allen walking across the bridge, heading towards the cruise ship, Allen handed the ticket to the cashier. The border patrol looked on but did not stop him. He crossed onto the boat with the other fourteen students. He found his four-bunk cabin and saw three other exchange students that he had not met. They introduced themselves and began to talk of their plans for the night.

"Are you going to the Duty Free tonight?" Scott, a tall thin man from Norway asked.

"What is the Duty Free?" Allen asked.

"That's where they have all types of liquor, beer and other items were you don't have to pay taxes on the purchase. It's much cheaper than what you normally pay." Scott told him.

"I might go just to see how much cheaper things are; I'm not much of a drinker."

Allen made his way to the duty-free part of the ship. It was overflowing with customers. Many of them, his classmates, were buying alcohol by the cases. Even reserved Steffan had a liter of vodka in his hands. Allen bought three loose beers.

Everyone went into their rooms to let the drink fest begin. By the fifth hour of the ten hour cruise, from Turku to Stockholm, every one of the exchange students was lit; Allen included, due to him drinking some of the Norwegians duty-free vodka. Allen found Steffan; face down in the middle of the ships hallway. He had drunk a liter of Absolute Vodka, solo, within a span of an hour and a half.

"The boy must want to kill himself," Allen thought, as he pried Steffans hand from the neck of the Vodka bottle. Allen helped Steffan off the floor and walked him towards the cabin. He knocked on the door. Someone answered within a few seconds.

"This guy needed some help." Allen told the man who answered the door. Steffan shifted over as he began to stand. He stumbled for a moment forward and began a lazy, drunken speech.

"What you say, Allen? You think you can out drink me?" Steffan pointed to himself sloppily. "You think, you so cool?" Allen dismissed the comment.

"Man, forget this. Yo, you need to go to sleep. I'll talk to you tomorrow." Allen turned away from the door and headed for his room. Upon passing the observation deck, he glanced at the time, three a.m. The boat was set to dock within the next four hours.

*

The Life and Times of Allen Court

Allen walked off the boat alone. He wanted to get a view of the city solo. While walking around he was surprised to see so many people of different ethnic backgrounds around him. People of all nationalities walked the streets. Stockholm, the city seemed to blanket a nation of exiles. The fashions were fast; the streets were alive with young people window shopping and along the sidelines, people watched each other all day. Allen loved the relaxed feel of the crowded, cobbled stoned streets. The streets were alive with contradictions that would make ones eyes swell. A tall blond Swedish woman walked hand in hand with a dark African prince.

Street vendors balked at low prices and haggled for the pretty girls' attention. Tourists were in a picture snapping frenzy, shooting frames of monuments and people. Street artist peddled colorful paintings in wooden frames. One man stood showing off his imitation Picasso to a young Swedish couple. While walking around Allen ran into a young East-Indian woman, he asked her where it would be good to eat at.

"Take the train until you reach this stop called Gamla Stan. There, you will find what you want. " She told him. Allen thanked her and walked to the subway stop.

"I probably won't see too many fine brown skinned women like that today," he thought getting on the train. By the time he reached his destination, he realized how wrong he was. The city was more diverse than he had ever imagined. Attractive woman of all nationalities flooded the subway cars and streets. "Now I see why those dudes where so happy about this place."

At Gamla Stan, the aroma of the open-air restaurants grabbed his attention. Allen spied over three restaurants before choosing a Greek kebab restaurant.

After eating, he returned to sight seeing. A young black man with long dreads walked toward him.

"Maybe this guy can direct me to a place where I can get my hair locked," he thought before stopping him.

"Excuse me; do you know where I can get someone to look at my hair here?" Allen asked.

"There's a hair salon right down this street further but it's not open yet." The man spoke with a heavy British accent. "You are from the States?"

"Yeah, and you?"

"London, England." The man said.

"An English Bloke." Allen joked. "My name's Allen."

"Martin." The two shook hands.

"Do you live here or are you just visiting?" Allen asked him.

"I have been living here, off and on, for over three years. I travel back and forth a lot? How did you get here?" Martin asked.

"I'm going to school in Finland. I'm here for only a day with a few other students. It's a whole lot of nice looking women out here. How are they?"

The man laughed.

"You will find out soon enough. They are very nice. You, being from the U.S., you won't have any problems here." Martin told him.

"Really?" Allen asked in disbelief. "I wish I had more time to hook something up here."

"Don't be surprised if you do. Some girls may invite you to stay with them."

"Come on now, for real?" Allen replied in disbelief.

"Just spend some time here, you'll see."

"I guess." Allen shrugged it off. "Where is the place again?" The man pointed the way. He thanked him before walking away. Allen circled the streets going in and out of clothing stores. "Nice gear," he thought as he passed the window of an urban clothing store. The girl behind the counter caught his eye.

Allen flirted with the cashier girl for a good ten minutes before some of his original travel companions spotted him. One chastised him.

"We looked up and down for you. We went up to the top of the boat. Looking for you! Never go off with out telling someone where you are."

"Tell you where I'm?" Allen did not know if his concern was sincere but still didn't like being talked to like a kid.

"You must not do that."

"I'm glad you're concerned, but I'm a grown man." Allen walked to where the other student's were shopping.

"We're about to get something to eat you want to come with us?" Julian asked.

"Yeah, that sounds good."

They walked around observing the sights. A curvaceous, Swedish girl walked by. All the men broke their necks turning to watch her glide pass them. The girls' ample hips swayed from side to side. The group could not hold back their comments.

"She got that backwards's' going." Allen commented.

"Is she a dime or a nickel?" Julian asked with a grin.

"That's a dime! Some of them are dimes and some are nickels." Allen looked on for one last glance. "I don't know what they been feeding these girls over here."

"They've been drinking milk." Fernando laughed.

"Yeah, milk and hayseed." Julian finished. They walked along coming in front of a huge, gray statue. As they waited in front of tall glass doors to a mall-like entrance, Emily pointed in the direction of the doors.

"We can eat in here." The group took the escalator. As they went down they descended into circular food court. All of the tables were filled with other young, twenty something college aged students eating and conversing all around them. Numerous restaurants contained foods ranging from Thai to Mexican. Taking a glance around the room, Allen was overwhelmed with the variety of beautiful women around them. Mark from Germany commented upon the looks.

"It's not like this in Finland. Why couldn't I have gone to school in Sweden?" He asked a loud. Every man in earshot nodded in agreement.

"I can just watch these girls go by all day." Julian said. His eyes were fixed on a Spanish beauty sitting alone at a table.

Allen saw a group of pretty Ethiopian girls sitting at a table.

"This is the spot. This is the spot. If I come back; No, when I come back. I'm coming right here!" Allen told them.

Emily and the two French girls left the group in search of food. Allen and the rest followed suit.

Allen had settled for some Mexican food. He stood with Julian and Mark looking for a table. Mark shuffled up next to him.

"Hey. Hey." He said excitedly in a hushed whisper. Those girls have been looking at you." He pointed to three girls next to him. A cute black girl sat with a grin. Her blond and dark haired girlfriends also were making motions in his direction.

"You should say something to them." Mark insisted. Allen took his advice and walked over to their table.

"May I sit here?" He asked calmly. The blond nodded with a smile while the black girl began giggling across the table to her dark haired friend.

"Where are you from," The dark haired girl asked? He noticed her large blazing, brown eyes.

"The U.S. and you?"

"I'm from Poland, I'm Elana." The girl extended her hand.

"I've been in Warsaw."

"Really that is where I was born. How was it?" Elana asked.

"I was too tired, and had too little time, to see it for real." He turned to the African girl.

"And you? Where are you from?" He asked.

"I'm from Tanzania. I'm Helen." The girl said with pride shaking his hand. Her honey-brown complexion shined with her wide smile. "And this here is Lisa. She is the only one from Sweden. You're with all those people?"

"What are you doing here?" They asked.

"You can say it's a sight-seeing tour. We go to school in Finland."

"Finland?" Helen replied with her amused grin. "Why did you go to school over there? It would have been much better with us here."

"Me, and all of my friends agree. Don't worry. I'll come to visit."

Allen continued making small talk before Mark came over to let him know they were leaving. "As fine as they are, I'm not going to push up on them." Allen got up from the table. "It was nice meeting you."

"I hope you enjoy yourself while you are here," the Swedish girl said as he got up to leave.

"I have been so far."

"The girls want to shop." Julian informed them as they filed along the streets. He walked close to

Madeline. The olive-complexioned French girl smiled at him. A tall African man in American clothes walked by. Madeline pointed towards him.

"He looks like he is from American." She told him.

"He's not." Allen said casually.

"How can you tell?" She asked.

"I can recognize it."

They stood in front of a mall-like store with large escalators. People crowded in and out of the store like a human ant farm. The clothing in the windows caught the groups' attention. Allen looked around and was impressed by the clothes. They had the typical sleek European style to them. He bought a T-shirt before leaving. Going solo again, he moved away from the group.

"Now where did that dred tell me to go?"

~

Allen walked up the increasingly crowded street. After walking around he found an African hair braiding shop.

He stepped inside the hair salon. A boisterous, African man cut a thin Somalian man's hair.

"Excuse me, but do you lock hair here." He asked a woman that was sitting behind the counter. The woman nodded yes. The chubby African man turned to listen in on the conversation.

"How much do you charge?" Allen asked. Before the woman could give him an answer, the fat man replied.

"For you. You, American? You want it done here? One hundred dollar."

"What?" Allen said in shock.

63

"One hundred dollar bill." The man repeated loudly.

"This dude is fronting, talking about a hundred dollars," he thought. "It doesn't cost that much at home." Allen told him.

"One hundred dollar bill." He repeated.

"I'm in Sweden he should be coming at me with Kroners or what else they say krowns, not dollars. But since I'm American he wants to charge me more. I'm out!" Let me get something to eat before it gets too late." Allen thought to himself frustrated.

*

Allen walked into the same kebab restaurant he had visited earlier that day and ordering the same meal as before. He scoffed the food down, while his eyes looked at the clock along the wall. "I got to get back soon." He rushed outside after eating the meal and took the train back to the harbor. Upon reaching the boat, large crowds of people waited to board. He scanned the back of the crowd not seeing anyone from his school. "Did they return yet or maybe they're closer towards the front?" He walked forward still not able to see anyone. He felt his heart skip.

"Where is this coming from?" He hugged his chest and sat down to collect himself. After a moment, he started to feel better. A tall heavy-set African woman came and sat down next to him. She was in her late twenties. Her braided extensions hung near to the middle of her back.

"Somalian," he thought as he looked over the features of her face.

She wore a thin dress that twisted lightly around her smooth, brown skin. Allen caught her eye, she nodded a hello.

"Excuse me, would you know a place here in Stockholm where people can lock hair." He asked.

"Yes, I do. Actually, my friend here can make it for you easy."

"Your friend?" Allen asked.

"Yeah. She is coming on this trip. "

"You're going to Finland?"

"No. We're going only to the islands in between the countries." She told him turning her head. She looked towards the entrance. He followed her eyes to see a thin, dark-complexioned African woman approaching

"Here she is. I will ask her to do it. Maybe she will do it on the boat. By the way, my name is Keisha." She extended her hand. He shook it, introducing himself. The woman was directly in front of them. Keisha introduced the woman to him as Ashtu.

The friendliness displayed by Keisha was lost upon Ashtu. She looked down at Allen arrogantly with blood-shot eyes. Her crocodile retinas scanned over him warily. She wore a long black weave that passed over her bony shoulders.

"I'm not receiving good vibes off this woman." Keisha and Ashtu began having a conversation in Swedish. Keisha would break in with words in English.

"But he is our brother." Allen heard Keisha saying, Ashtu shook her head no. Ashtu then turned her attention to him.

"You want your hair locked," She asked him?

"If you wouldn't mind," Allen told her. She looked him over again.

"I can do it for say, four hundred crowns." Ashtu said as Keisha objected. The horn blew for the passengers to board. Allen stood up to go.

"Four hundred crown is about 50 dollars. At least she is talking in her money. I can pay her." Keisha stood up with him.

"Come to our cabin after you get settled in. It's on the second floor." Keisha whispered. "I'll talk with her."

~

Allen came to their cabin later. On the way; he bumped into Steffan. Steffan had spent the entire day, sleeping under a tree. "The coordinator of the trip spent the whole day with a hangover, his head on a rock. To each his own," Allen thought moving on. He bought a bottle of rum for Ashtu and some vodka for Keisha. Ashtu seemed satisfied, yet looked upon him suspiciously. Keisha talked happily as Ashtu worked. They asked him how long had he been in town. Once he told them only for the day, Keisha began insisting he return.

"When are you returning to Stockholm?" Keisha asked.

"I don't know?" He told her. "I would like to come back."

"Yes, brother. You must come back very soon." Keisha said.

"If you like, you can stay with me." Ashtu said. Allen nearly jumped backwards.

"All this time she has not given me the slightest indication she even likes me. What brought this on," he thought?

"Yes." Keisha chimed in. "You can stay with one of us. We both live near each other in Fittja. You can have more time to visit the city."

"All right, that will help me come back faster." They exchanged telephone numbers.

"Are you going to the party tonight?" Keisha asked.

"No. I'm going to rest." He told them.

"Be safe on your return and be sure to call." Keisha reminded him as he got up to leave.

He thanked them for the offer and returned to his room. "London Dred was right," he thought returning to his cabin. "I'll be coming back soon."

Chapter 7
Would you be happy

Upon entering Finland there were problems. The other students floated passed the border guards without a care in the world but the guards stopped Allen. He was not surprised. The rest of his group walked by while he had to turn over his passport to the guard. The guard examined his passport.

"What's wrong with him," Allen thought? The guard handed his passport back not looking at him.

Allen walked through the port heading towards the same waiting port as the day before. He waited in line and asked for a cup of water. A large woman behind the counter gave him the smallest cup of water available then she held out her other hand showing three fingers.

"I didn't have to pay for water yesterday, but it's not even worth fighting over." Her face turned downward in a frown as he paid her. The tables were all open. The exchange students were spread throughout the room. Allen took a seat at a lone table. Alongside him two French students sat. He put his bag along the table. The woman from the counter continued to stare at him, her look became nastier by the moment. He chose to ignore her, and began to write a letter.

The angry cashier walked up to his table. She pointed to a folded paper in the middle of the table. When he looked to see what she was pointing towards, she grabbed his camera bag. Allen grabbed her hand and snatched his camera bag from her.

"What's your problem?" He yelled, the other students now turned to see what was going on. "I can't even bother with it now." Julian and Emily sat next to him.

"What happened," they asked? He explained that she came over and just tried to grab his bag.

"I would have moved if that was the thing but…she tried to grab my camera and wasn't having it." He told them.

"Something's wrong with her." Julian told him. "Anyway, we are leaving in another twenty minutes to take the train back." Julian told him.

"Cool." Allen told him, they left moments later.

*

Saga had called him the day after he returned from Stockholm. He told her of the people he met and what had happened on the trip. She asked him if he needed any help with his language classes and was appreciated the assistance. She began to come over ever other week to help him with memorizing and formulating sentences in her native language. He had noticed that she was fast becoming a constant friend in his life. He opened up and began to speak to her about his relationship with Cynthia. At first, he noticed a discomfort when he mentioned her name but later on, she placed her discomfort aside and gave Allen the advice she think he needed. She gave him her opinion of what the situation called for. She constantly spoke in terms that women in love often do, "if you love her, then you should go be with her."

This, was the impossible quagmire for Allen.

"How do I get to her?" Allen would ask. Saga told him plainly, "If you can come all the way here, You will find a way to get to where she is?" Allen knew she had a point. But how to keep from being distracted and finding the money to get to Egypt was another story. Yes, it had been cheap to travel through Europe, so far, but the East? This was going to take some major planning. Something Allen was not quite up to task at the time. He wanted some peace so he told Saga after a long study session he needed some time to think.

Allen lay in bed contemplating what his life could be like if he could focus his energy and time on obtaining his goals. "I need to stop playing the dream out in my head." He told himself. He pulled himself up from the covers.

Allen began to think that life was meaningless and the only joy was in the pleasures he could indulge in for the moment. He shook the thought away from his head.

"I need to manifest a higher dream. I need to get a girlfriend. But who? Cynthia is so far away I don't know how to get to her. It only frustrates me to think about it. It has always been hit and miss with her. Besides, she has too much of an affect on me. I got feelings and I do care about her, but I don't know how to make a relationship work.'

The phone rang. He was surprised to hear Raheem's raspy voice.

"What's up?" Raheem asked.

"Nothing. What's up with you?"

"Man, I'm calling because of this rapper. You remember that one Finnish kid I was trying to teach his lines."

"That skinny kid in the blue camouflage, I met at Bounce?"

"Yeah, him. He is trying to pull out of this concert we've been rehearsing. I need you to replace him."

"What?" Allen said in disbelief. "Replace him? What do you mean replace him?"

"I need somebody for this Friday, in Tampere."

"This Friday? It's Tuesday. I don't know any of your songs nor do I even know where Tampere is?"

"Tampere is a few hours south of here. You can do this. All you have to do is learn the hooks." Raheem insisted.

"Hooks, man.. i don't know. I ain't happy with none of this."

"What could make you happy?"

"I'd be happy if I could fly to the moon, take some binocular frames, put the lens on zoom. And see in my life the things I didn't see. And be the type of light that escapes gravity. That would make me happy." Allen said in an instant.

"See I knew you got it in you. All that metaphysical stuff."

"Whatever, I guess I can do it, but, wait…." Allen agreed just to get him off the phone but decided to ask…."Hey, I need about 500 fin mark for that night."

"Done deal. I'll come by on Wednesday, we can work on the hooks. Talk to you."

'Where there is a will there is a way.' Allen thought. Now if I start saving the haircut money with some other hustle money I'll have enough money for this trip." Allen smiled for a moment. Wait, how much money for this move will be the next thing I need to find out. I'll stop by a travel agency before my sports class tomorrow.

Meshawn Deberry

~

"These cats have never played baseball." Allen observed as a man crossed his arms over the bat. He tried pointing some basics out to Raul. Timing was important in the swing; still Raul swung a second too early at a lofted pitch. "My turn," Allen thought holding the bat loosely. Daniel wound up throwing to him as the Finnish instructor kept a close watch.

"Muy Lejos!" Allen shouted to Daniel lifting the bat in the direction over the fence.

Daniel laughed as he threw the ball. Allen swung, hitting it in perfect timing as it came over the base. The smack from the ball caught the student's attention as it continued to rise in the sky falling well behind the fence. Allen laughed out loud.

"See."

Kru, the instructor, walked over to Allen.

"That was a very good but the point of *pesapallo,* is not to hit the ball as far as you can as American baseball."

"I won't hit it so far next time." Allen told him.

"We're going to move onto playing catch." Kru yelled, to the class to pick a glove and partner up.

The class formed two lines standing twenty feet from each other. The instructor went down the line handing out baseballs to the group for practice. Daniel stood across from Allen. They practiced the drills. Kru told them a little about the game Pesapallo.

"This is a Finnish game. Many of our games have kept us in shape and are somehow associated with war. This game is very much like American baseball." Kru motioned towards Allen. "But the object is not to hit the ball as far as you can. We don't say 'outs,' we call catches, kills and certain hits, depending on where you move to, wounds. We hit the ball within a perimeter set up within the field and actually if you hit it outside the perimeter we say you are killed."

They played the game for a moment before going in for the day. The next three classes, the instructor informed them, would cover the game. Allen had stopped by small travel agency before the class. After learning the prices for flights, Allen realized that he had enough money to cover getting there. The real issue now was to fulfill his school obligation. "Cynthia, I may be seeing you after all." He thought being inspired by the vision.

*

Friday came sooner than expected for Allen. He found himself in the backseat of a crowed four-door Saab on the way to Tampere. Raheem had asked him to perform with him and he did his best under the circumstances. The show had gone better than Allen had expected. He remembered most of the lines; even with only last minute instructions. The crowd moved along to the music. Allen was surprised at how diverse the group of people was at the show.

On the ride back to Jyvaskyla Allen was feeling the fire. He had heard how easy it was travel through countries and now could see the possibilities. He had managed to make some friends who shared his love of hip-hop music. For the moment, he felt he was starting to see some daylight.

Chapter 8
A Love Supreme

"I wonder if our American brother is going to come back." Keisha said to her friend Akili and Ashtu. They sat in Keisha's living room drinking vodka.

"He's not any brother of mine." Ashtu complained.

"Don't say that." Keisha said. "He is black, strong and handsome."

"Well, I don't like him. He didn't pay me what I wanted to make his hair Rasta." She said angrily.

"He did give you something." Keisha said. "Besides, it's not always about money." Keisha tried to tell Ashtu.

"No. It's always about money when it comes to Ashtu." Akili said. The three started to laugh. "I would like to meet him. What did you say his name was?" Akili asked.

"Allen." Keisha said. "It would be good to have an American friend. Maybe he could get us some clothes and other things from America." The three nodded in agreement. The phone rang; Keisha went to pick it up.

"Hi, it's Allen."

"Hey, brother how are you." Keisha smiled. "We were just speaking about you. Are you coming back this way anytime soon?"

"That's why I was calling. I want to know if it's possible for me to stay with you if I come next week. I might have one friend with me as well."

"You two can stay with me," Keisha replied. "I have enough room for two people. How long do you think you will stay?"

"About four days. We should arrive on Thursday and leave on Monday."

"That's fine with me." Keisha agreed while Ashtu shook her head. "My friends here say hello to you" Keisha said loudly.

"I want to meet him." Akili said loudly setting down her drink. Allen could hear the commotion in the background.

"Tell her we'll meet soon."

"I will do that brother, you take care."

~

Cynthia sat in her room reading over various email messages. She kept her eye out for one in particular. Allen's message had yet to be received. Her grandfather had told her about the chance meeting on the plane. Sure that today was the day. She still had not heard anything from him.

"They say patience is a virtue but waiting for you has become more like vice. When are you going to call," She thought? Cynthia looked at a picture frame with the two of them together. "It's always tomorrow with you." She left the room, leaving the computer on.

*

Allen sat in his Finnish classroom, bored as ever. Daydreaming about Zaleha and a host of other girls; women flowed through his mind like a river.

"How many have you seen this week," he thought? "Too many." He answered himself. "Which

74

one means something to you? The one I can't reach," he continued, "my conscious is getting the best of me."

His Finnish language instructor brought up a class assignment that took him for a ride. The instructor marched left to right in front of the classroom

"I want you to write about something very close to you. Yourselves." The Finnish teacher said, as she stood in the middle of the class room. "I want you to write about what you believe. The things that make you who you are. Then when you are done, I want you to translate it into our language."

"Why do you want us to write this?" A student asked.

"If you write about something, or someone close to you, you'll remember the words. This assignment will be one page long. It is due next week."

She dismissed the class.

Allen took the assignment home. He decided to mellow out before he sat down to write. He searched through his cd collection before finding the most appropriate selection. Coltrane's-*A Love Supreme*, blasted out of his speakers. Notes that sprang from the edge of the universe cut the silence of the room. Allen wrote his name out constantly as the tenor saxophone wailed over the stereo speakers. Allen Court - How can I articulate the sound the world wants to hear? He wrote setting his hands in motion. Remembering the words that his teacher had said, he began to write.

"I define my self through one thought. Just to let the world feel it so they can see, better yet, so they can know it came from a common man. Starting something and willing to let it create a new life. If it's a new love, then so be it. If it's Cynthia, then let it be. Speaking on what I believe in. A love supreme I had to bring it to my life. A love supreme, I had to let it be my name. Writing about what I believe in, I have my faith in god and I believe in me." He looked over it and thought. "Now, how am I going to translate this?"

The phone rang, breaking him from his writing. "Hello."

"Yo, wassup playboy." Raheem said, "What are you up to."

"Just doing some homework, what's going on with you?"

"I'm about to go to the club. Seeing if you want to come?"

"Yeah, I would like to go."

"Get Daniel to come too."

"All right." Allen hung up the phone. He returned to his paper, reading over the lines. "Cynthia? Why did she jump up in to this? I can't ignore it. Should I give her a call?" He thought to himself. "I've been putting it off for a while now and the truth is I miss her. Maybe I should call." He took out the number that Malik had given him. He walked over to the phone. "Nawwh, man. If she wanted to talk, she could call me. What if she is with some dude right now? Ahhh no. Nope, I just need to let her go." Allen began to walk away from the phone. "Damn, I miss her in my life." He walked back over to phone dialing the numbers. He punched in the digits. The phone rang four times before anyone picked up.

"Hello." The voice on the other end said.

"Hey, is Cynthia in?" Allen asked.

"Allen, is that you?" He heard the excitement in her voice.

"You know it. How are you?"

"A little tired from studying, but other than that, I'm all right. My grandfather let me know that you had run into each other on the plane."

"Yeah, he gave me your number."

"He told me. So you finally decided to make that move." She said.

"If the world is ours might as well do the right thing by it." Allen told her. Cynthia laughed.

"I see your confidence hasn't gone anywhere."

"Sometimes it's a little slower with some people."

There was a slight silence. Allen shook his head at himself. "Man, I should have called her sooner, now she thinks that I don't care." He thought.

"You know this is long distance and all." Allen joked trying to break the silence.

"It's all long distance. Anyways, I'm glad that you called. Giving me a chance to say something I've wanted to say."

"What's that," Allen asked?

"I miss you."

"I miss you, too. I'm sorry for taking so long its' just that….."

"What? Too many distractions? Have you seen enough places, enough sites, girls?" She asked, with Allen pausing. He began to wonder why she was hinting at things but let it go.

"I have to leave soon. I'm meeting some friends of mine here. I'll be in touch, look for me."

"Not, today?" She whispered.

"No. But, tomorrow."

"I will. Goodbye."

He hung up the phone.

~

Bounce had been newly renovated. The bar stood in the middle of the club. All of the foreign exchange students bought drinks standing at the edge of the bar. Hip hop music blasted through the speaker system. Allen was among the foreign group talking and drinking.

He brief conversation with Cynthia was still in the back of his head. "She is so far away. It would be next to impossible to have a relationship with so much distance between us."

He ordered another beer and opted to get out on the dance floor. He moved around for a moment but couldn't catch half the feeling as he normally could. Leaving the dance floor, he chose to sit in the back of the club. Daniel arrived and Allen told him about the up coming trip. Daniel had agreed with the arrangements for Stockholm. Allen mingled with a few more people before ending the night, taking a cab back to his apartment.

Chapter 9
Scarlen

A week had gone by since Allen spoke with Cynthia. Classes had moved on smoothly, he finalized plans to see Keisha in Stockholm. Daniel looked forward to going since he didn't go with the first group.

Allen and Daniel left Thursday morning for Stockholm. They packed their clothes and set out at five o'clock in the morning to catch the train to Turku, Finland. There, they would have a ten hour cruise to Sweden.

While walking behind Daniel, Allen looked up at the sky and was amazed at how bright the stars shown at night. "On top of the world, or at least close."

They reached the train station sooner than expected and waited with a few other groggy passengers for the train. When it arrived, the two fell asleep as soon as they placed their bags down.

"Nothing left to do but ride along and wait," Allen thought falling asleep.

*

"I really like this." Daniel said peering out past the ship's deck. They had slept a couple of hours on the boat and woke up early to take a walk around the ship; then settled into a lounge area where people slowly drifted in. Some poor lounge acts sang American B-hits from the eighties and popular Finnish and Swedish folk music. It was becoming unbearable for Allen. He pulled his CD changer from his camera bag.

"What music do you have?" Daniel asked. Daniel began to leaf through his CDs selecting one. Allen picked a song and waited for the intro. Daniel held his hand out for the headphones, waiting to listen.

"I'll let you hear in a minute." Allen told him.

After the song faded out Allen handed the CD player over to Daniel. While Daniel was listening; he turned from him, then back to the sea. The other cruise ships and trade boats sailed by, he could tell that Daniel was trying to interpret the lyrics. Allen watched the passing ships.

"To yearn." Daniel spoke. "To yearn is to want. To want for something that will not be yours?"

"Yeah, I like that translation."

"But you will still try to have it anyway." Daniel finished staring at the CD case. "What else you have?"

Daniel leafed through his CDs and found another classic. "You love these oldies, don't you?" Allen asked putting in another classic CD. Daniel was trying to decipher the music but had trouble trying to catch all the different tones that were constantly changing. Daniel shook his head taking the headphones off.

"I got nothing." Daniel continued shaking his head

"Finish the beer so we can go outside."

Daniel nodded in agreement to this and finished the drink. They walked to the top of the ship and stepped outside a side exit. The wind started to blow so strongly that many of the passengers who walked out on deck turned right back around. Determined not to let the wind keep them from their destination, they continued walking. Daniel wanted to go the bow but was obstructed with some bars. He started to climb over one of the bars.

"Where the hell you're going? This ain't Titanic. You fall over, you're gonna die! Get back over here." Allen insisted.

Daniel shuffled back over the rail.

"What's wrong with you?" Allen asked Daniel. Daniel laughed walking back around the side of the ship. The boat slowly drifted pass small islands. Along the banks of the shore, large, gray boulders bordered the deep, green bushes and thick trees. Brick mansions along were nestled along the forested area. Allen had not clearly seen the peacefulness of this on his first trip with the group of foreign students. While looking out, Daniel pointed to a beige dog running along the edge of an island. A large house stood elevated on a hill area where two little children played in the back yard. Daniel was impressed by the scene.

"Isn't that what every man wants;" Daniel asked looking at Allen. "To have a house, a wife, some kids and a dog?"

Allen first response was to laugh at the way the question was asked but then was struck with the seriousness of the question. He only stared further at the place while it was still in his sight. Allen did not answer him openly. He looked on and nodded, finally realizing the intelligence of the question.

"Yes, it is." Allen said respectfully. 'But, I don't know when it's going to be my time,' he thought. Allen took out his camera and took a photo of the passing island.

~

The ships horn began to blow, alerting the passengers to the ships soon arrival. Allen and Daniel had sat in a waiting area watching as the ship came closer to the harbor. The sun had set an hour ago marking the time half past seven. Keisha had agreed to pick them up a little after eight. The ship dragged along, making a hard turn in the water. Allen had heard this same sound on the last trip, but now, understood what was happening. Daniel had busied himself with making friends with a plump, Danish girl. Daniel returned with his head in the air.

"You see. You see?"

"You get her number? You know big girls need love too!"

"She is very nice, don't you think?" Daniel asked.

"Yeah, she's cute. But you better eat your Wheaties." Allen told him.

"What? Repeat to me, please. I, don't understand?"

"Forget it." Allen wanted to check on Keisha. "We need to get out of here." They strolled through the main hull going across a thick metallic walkway. It reminded Allen of the airplane boarding walkway; all white until they reached the opening, where it turned blue. Three custom's agents stood waiting, taking various

81

passengers aside to be checked. Allen and Daniel walked through with only a glance from the agents. At the bottom of the stairs, groups of people hugged love ones. Outside, people unloaded their cases of duty- free beer and alcohol into cars. Allen looked around but didn't see Keisha or Ashtu.

"Maybe she's a little late." Then he heard a familiar voice shouting out loud.

"Allen." He turned to see Keisha moving towards him arms outstretched.

"Brother, how are you?" Keisha asked, happy to see him.

"I'm fine. This here is my friend from school I was telling you about." Daniel went and shook Keisha's hand. Allen was glad that she had arrived.

"Where is Ashtu? She's here isn't she?" Allen asked.

"She is out in the car. Come, Come." Allen lunged behind her, following her through the sliding doors outside. Daniel was right behind him. A middle aged, African man with a bald head and black horn rimmed glasses met them outside. Keisha introduced Carl, as Ashtu's friend. They placed their bags in the back of his dark blue Audi. Keisha took the passenger seat leaving Allen and Daniel to sit in the back. Ashtu calmly sat behind the driver. Daniel slid in the middle and Allen directly behind Keisha. Allen introduced Daniel to Ashtu but she rolled her eyes at him. Her mouth was plastered in a dark brown lipstick and her eyes were bloodshot red. She looked Allen in the eyes then his hair.

"What's going on, Ashtu." Allen asked.

"So you still want your hair to be done?"

"You're all business? Can I get a hello first?

"Hello." She said smiling with a crocodile grin. The car began to speed off.

"If you want to talk about it now, yeah." Allen told her. This was not the type of greeting that he expected.

"Six hundred Krowns."

"That is seventy five dollars." Allen wondered why she was so hard on him. Keisha tried to say something only to have her words shaken off with a wave of Ashtu's hand.

"Six hundred Krowns." She repeated.

"I don't see why you have to charge me that much?"

"Ashtu." Keisha interjected. "You know you can make it for free. He is our Brother. He is…" Ashtu began to speak to Keisha in Swahili. Daniel looked at them confused.

"We should talk about this later." Keisha said in English. Allen turned his attention to a large cathedral they were passing. One building they passed, Keisha told them, was the King's home. It was huge, cathedral style building with rows of large windows. He saw another large building standing nearly three stories high. On the building, along the awning, were gold letters.

"What is that?" He asked Keisha pointing in its direction.

"That's the Museum of Nobel." Daniel turned around to catch a fleeting glimpse of it out the back window.

"We should go there." Daniel said. "Possibly tomorrow." Allen nodded.

The car swerved onto the highway. The city lights soon surrounded the car as it drifted on the road. The lights reminded him of an American city. An upbeat, West African melody played on the tape deck. The drum beat patted a constant rhythm that matched the voice of the baritone singer. The car turned off the highway and etched up a street going underneath a walkway until it

83

reached a parking lot filled with kiosks. Allen looked to see a gyro place alongside a closed supermarket. The surrounding area was filled with trees.

"Fittja." Keisha said proudly.

"This is it. Let's go." Ashtu opened her door getting out. She spoke with Carl in Swedish while the others went to the trunk for their bags. Carl came out of the car and opened the trunk. Allen thanked him for the ride and began to follow Keisha. Keisha gave Carl a kiss on the cheek telling him to come by Akili's apartment for a party. Keisha walked on, while Ashtu focused on another desire.

"You're going to stay with Keisha for the night. You can bring your things to my place tomorrow." Ashtu told Allen without feeling. Allen had originally been assured by Ashtu that he could stay over her place but judging by her cold and aloofness; he took these words as a blessing.

"That's cool." Allen told her. Ashtu turned and said a few words in Swedish to Keisha; then waved goodbye to Allen and Daniel.

"Where's she going?" Daniel asked.

"Home. She lives two buildings down." Keisha told them as they walked past the small kiosks. They turned right and walked past a lively bar. There was a pizza place that caught Allen's attention. A group of Armenian youths walked past them. A drunken black man staggered out of the bar and caught the eye of one of the larger Armenians. He pointed and began laughing, causing the other three boys to start yelling at the drunk. A middle-aged Arabian stepped out of the bar and helped the staggering man to the edge of the parking lot.

"This is the ghetto." Keisha laughed out loud. They walked passed a two story building. Keisha pointed up to a window.

"That is Akili's place; after you drop off your

things we will pick her up and get something to eat."
Keisha told him.

"Is this where a lot of foreigners live?" Asked
Allen

"Yes, near the outskirts of town."

"How long does it take to get to town from
here?" Allen looked as they crossed over the bridge's
walkway. From this distance, he could see the train
pulling into the Fittja station.

"About fifty minutes to reach the center." After
she said this Daniel tugged at Allen's arm.

"Maybe we should find out a hotel that is closer."

"If you want? We can do that tomorrow. Let's
just hang out and meet some people." They had reached
Keishas' building and waited in front of the elevator.
They went one flight up and rang on Akili's door. A
short, petite African woman opened the door. Upon
seeing Keisha, she broke into a wide smile.

"Sister!" The small woman said in a strong, rich
voice.

"How are you, Akili?" Keisha asked.

"Good, Good. Come in."

Akili welcomed all, waving them into her
apartment. Keisha introduced everyone to Akili. Daniel
showed an interest in Akili. She was an attractive older
woman with a curvaceous shape. She took their coats,
turning to sliding closet that had mirrors along the front.

Allen leaned in poking fun at Daniel.

"She looks a lot better than that Danish girl, ehh?'

"Si, Si." Daniel responded. Allen laughed as they
took off their shoes and walked in the living room. There
was a blue leather sofa with a large television across from
it. Allen and Daniel stood in the center of the living
room; Keisha motioned for them to join her in the
kitchen. They walked into a small, but neat kitchen with a
white table in front of the window. They could see

people who approached before they reached the door. Akili went to the cupboard and picked out three large glasses which she filled with beer before passing them around. Allen sat down at the table, accepting the glass. Daniel tried to decline by waving his hand but with a pat on the back by Keisha, he relaxed and accepted the drink. By the looks of a half-finished beer before her, Akili had already started before they're arrival. The initial conversation revealed their countries of origin. Keisha was from Somalia, and had lived in Sweden for over seven years. She spoke of being a slim girl upon arrival and how over the years, she had gained a little weight. Akili had come from Tanzania and had lived in Stockholm for over nine years. They continued speaking for a few hours more before calling it a night.

"Tomorrow, I will go sight-seeing." Daniel told him.

"What time?" Allen asked.

"I will leave out at seven."

"That early? Wake me up when you leave."

*

Tomorrow came and went for Allen. Daniel did leave out at seven, allowing Allen to sleep in. He awoke around noon leaving Keisha's place for Akili's. Akili invited him outside to her balcony. He spent most of the day talking to her and was impressed by her warmness. After only a day, he felt as if she was a close relative. Akili brought up Asthu.

"Have you been to her apartment?" Akili asked. Allen shook his head no.

"She is the one who first invited me out but now has no time."

"No matter." Akili said. "Tonight, we cook and have a party here; then we go out. This time to a club called 'Savannah.' You will like it there." A smile gleamed from her face.

~

Food sat steaming on the kitchen counter. Spinach dressing, hand rolled tortillas and chicken made with a rich marinara sauce, flooded Allen nostrils with delicious smells. He ate the food, feeling his strength replenished as he savored over the new tastes. Keisha and Akili had cooked traditional Somalian and Tanzanian food. The mix of flavors, combined with the liquor and high laughter, set the tone for the night. They took a cab to a bar; having a few more drinks before going to the nightclub.

They walked into "Club Savannah." Allen thought he was in heaven. Dream Ethiopian girls floated in and out of the various rooms. Lively, African reggae helped to move the crowd. Allen walked into one of the rooms to hear recent American hip-hop playing over the loud speakers. An ebony-colored Ethiopian girl walked passed drawing him into the main dance room. He went to her finding a place on the dance floor. They danced for a few minutes before leaving the floor. As she walked from the dance floor a shot of lust came over him as he looked over the shapely curve of her hips. She turned and flashed him a clear, white smile; the contrast was lovely with her glowing black skin. Her breast moved so firmly from side to side that it made his attention gravitate towards her body. She sat down at a table with three of her Ethiopian friends.

"This girl is it", Allen thought excited, barely holding his cool.

"I'm Allen." The girl looked at him smiling. She lifted her hand and ran it over the side of his face. "She has some sexy eyes," he thought. "Wait. She's not talking back? I got to spark some kind of conversation."

"This place is hot tonight," her smile remained. "I see you are here with your friends." The girl next to him leaned over the table.

"She arrived here from Ethiopia three weeks ago. She only speaks Tingrian." Allen felt as if a bomb had just exploded in his heart.

"No," He shook his head. The girls smiled widen. "Is she getting some pleasure from this?"

She leaned over and kissed him on the cheek, only increasing the pain;

"Found my queen and she can't even talk to me. It just was too good to be true." He stayed for a moment before moving on. He danced with Keisha and Akili and laughed at Daniel as he danced. He didn't make any more attempts at meeting anyone new at the club. He had endured enough disappointments for one night.

*

"Pull over up here." Keisha insisted. Carl obliged. They were in front of a world-famous burger restaurant. The crowds of people around the front door made it look like the entrance to a popular night club instead of fast food restaurant. Allen sat in the back seat, his eyes staring ahead. Suddenly, he looked to his right. Something made him notice her.

"Could you be the one I've been looking for?" Allen thought as he turned looking at a staring girl. She was surrounded by a group of women but his eyes only focused upon her. Her white trench coat made a sharp contrast with her raven-black, curly hair. The girls began pointing their hands in his direction.

"They're looking over here." Daniel said nodding at his friend.

"You thinking what I'm thinking?" He asked Daniel; Allen's pulse jumped at the sight of the cinnamon-skinned girl. Instinctively, he left the car. He could see the group of four where all attractive. "You all are fine, but you're the one I want."

He walked towards the short girl in the white coat.

"Where is she from? Is she mixed? Spanish, black, what?" Allen thought with Daniel trailing two steps behind him. "Wait a minute; please let this girl speak English. I don't want another "Savannah" incident." Catching up to her, he now stood directly in front of her. "Before I get my hopes up; let me ask."

"What's up?" The girls looked on in amused silence. "How are you?" He continued with the short girl smiling. "Do you speak English?" The girls looked at him and shook their heads no. "Well, why are they still smiling," he thought?

"No? No?" He asked in disbelief. "Well since you don't speak English, then it doesn't matter what I say. I'm going to keep talking." He began speaking to the whole group moving from face to face.

"I go to school in Finland, but I like Stockholm. Do you like Stockholm?" Allen paused asking the question with the tall, curly haired girl taking the bait, she shook her head yes. "She could be Eritrian or Ethiopian," he thought for a moment. Allen deduced that the girl on the side was a dark-haired Swede and the other South American. He still could not place the one he wanted to know.

"I'm Allen. And I'm from the US. This is my friend Daniel." The girls began laughing; Allen looked directly at the girl who caught his eye.

"Are you from here?"

The girl smiled, shaking her head no.

"So where are you from?"

89

The girl looked at her friends before answering in a slow Spanish voice, letting the sound of her town slip from her tongue.

"Malmo."

"Malmo?" What"s a Malmo?" Allen asked. The brown skinned girl turned to the tall African girl speaking in Swedish. Daniel elbowed Allen in the arm lifting his hands asking, what was going on?

"I don't know, just calm down."

The girl turned back to him.

"Where are you from?" She asked him.

"The U.S." Allen heard a honk turning to see Keisha returning to the car. "I gotta go. If you give me your number, we might be able to find some time to get together. Got a pen?" She shook her head no then began looking through her purse. She pulled out her lipstick writing her name on the back of a piece of paper.

"Scarlen." Allen read aloud. "I'll call you sometime tomorrow." Allen returned to the car with Daniel. Turning around as the car moved away Allen could see her waving goodbye.

~

Daniel walked along the dark harbor. The clouds blanketed the sky with a gray mist. Allen told him about the Vasa, a famous Swedish warship that capsized on its first day at sea. They agreed to head over after walking along the harbor, passing retired military warships along the dock. They walked on, coming to the Vasa Museum. Inside the multistory center, was the old ship hanging by cables from the rafters. The mahogany-brown wood of the ship was buffed to perfection, leaving a shine that reflected the light. The ship had life size mannequins performing ship hands daily routines. Along the floor, giant bronze canons with faces of roaring lions were positioned towards the crowd. These were the original cannons that were carried on the ship the day it went down. Allen walked around the ship amazed at the detailed attention given to the boats body. Crafted faces of lions roared from the bow. Allen stopped to read over the history of the ship. The king had made the Vasa, his head warship, dumping large amounts of money and years for the construction of it.

The Vasa was going to be the pride of the Swedish navy. Unfortunately, the architect who designed the ship had not taken in account the weight of the cannons that would be loaded on later. The back of the ship was too narrow for the additional weight to retain its buoyancy. On the crowning day of the launch, crowds of people came to watch their pride of the sea set sail; only to see it go down, swallowed in the water.

After leaving the museum, Allen called up Scarlen. They agreed to meet at the same as the night before.

"I'll see you later at Fittja," he told Daniel.

Allen met up with Scarlen and headed for the Greek kebab restaurant he was fond of. He talked endlessly with Scarlen, telling her many things. He looked over her pretty face noticing a small scar on her forehead. Instead of being a distraction for him it made him concerned. The food arrived, while Allen ate, she sat watching him intensely. Suddenly, she began to speak.

"Tell me something real? Tell me some part of you; some part that you hold inside?"

"I don't know what you mean?" He thought.

"I'm sorry. I've asked you so many questions and haven't revealed anything of myself; I've always been this way," she said.

"What will change you?" Allen asked Scarlen. She looked him in his eyes.

"Love." She said with out hesitation.

Allen felt his heart jump at her direct response. She sat quietly looking at him. "This could turn into something nice," he thought as she began to speak.

"Do you have any brothers, or sisters?" She asked.

"Yeah. I have a brother." His birthday is next week as a matter of fact. Scarlens' smile insisted he continue.

"I miss him." Allen paused for a moment.

"Have you..." she paused for a moment finding her words, "talked with him?" Allen shook his head no.

"I called home, no answer. I wish I could have talked with him before I came here." Allen looked into the mirror that lined the restaurant. "You can't tell him nothing; he reminds me of myself when I was that age. When I think of home, and family, I can see how much they influenced me now. But on another part I know it's up to me to go to the next level."

"What do you mean?" She asked. How can I explain my thoughts? Just tell her with your life.

"One of my uncles; around when I was a kid, about eleven years old, my uncle told me he was going to teach me how to shoot. It happened to be a shotgun. He did it just to see what would happen when I fell down. You know what I took with me from that moment? When you shoot but miss, get up, aim, brace yourself, breathe, and try again."

"And if you get it right, you'll hit." She finished for him.

"Exactly."

Scarlen laughed, tilting her head backwards, a strand of her raven colored hair slipped past her neck.

"And you? Do you have any brothers or sisters?"

"Yes. I have two brothers and two sisters."

Allen was captivated with the seductiveness of Scarlen; she held a quiet poise that was both mysterious yet inviting. Her glances dared him to come closer. Each moment he felt something deep inside him turning during the conversation.

"She is the first that can compete with Cynthia. The other girls I have met are nice but she could be something serious… no, no. Don't move so fast." Allen turned back to her with his questions.

"So your family, are they here or back home?"

"They're here."

"Are you the oldest? Youngest?"

"I'm the oldest."

While staring at her, he reached over to her face and lightly, traced the small scar that was barely visible on her cheek. The mark's olive color was a shade lighter than her honey-colored skin. The scar intensified his curiosity about Scarlen.

"How did that happen?" He asked.

"When I lived on the islands. I was playing with hmmm…," her small mouth stayed open, her tongue lightly touching her teeth.

"A machete. I was trying to cut this piece of wood," lifting her hand slowly she acted it out, "the blade was stuck. I pulled it hard and." She pretended to pull away her hand away; suddenly swinging her hand towards her face completing the action.

"Was anyone around to help?"

Scarlen giggled mischievously.

"Mi, Madre. She was yelling."

"That's crazy." Allen laughed.

"Tell me something about you. Tell me how you're parent's are or where like. How where you as a child?" Scarlen asked with Allen exhaling, took a moment to think of memories long ago.

He began speaking slowly at first then gathered momentum, speaking about himself in third person satire.

The Life and Times of Allen Court

"To go on further in A. Court's prehistory or… prenatal; whatever have you. His father, let the city tell it, was a no good, low down hustling man. A flashy "jive" talking 'slicksta,' who packed guns and bedded women as constant and consistent as the sun sets. Whispers of how, 'the apple could not fall far from the tree' spread like rumors with the birth of his newborn son. Crowning this one… Allen." Allen breathed in as Scarlen's mouth opened at his story. He continued…

"With all of the displeasure many held for Elder Court, his son rested on the opposite end of that magnetic pole. Generally, loved by all, especially his grandmother, he only caught hell from a few. One, who, for the life of him, could never figure out what his precious, baby sister, ever saw in a no-good, Court."

He took a breath while Scarlen smiled in amazement from the tempo of the story. Allen then changed it into first person phrases.

"My grandmother held me with the highest esteem, as she would coddle me, her sweet grandchild. Her preaching son would dismiss me as a hoodwinking, future hoodlum. Imagine, as the superlatives would fly…."

Entertained by Allen's vivid pictures of the past, Scarlen giggled. His mind raced out loud, pulling his words along.

"I passed time within the mist of conversations. I remember people, mostly relatives, or friends of the family, gathered in late night circles sometimes over half empty cans of beer, sometimes sober; complaining and contemplating their struggles away. Most conversations consisted of things like black man/white man politics; women; sports like Hearns versus Hagler; trickle down economics; money, (meaning the lack thereof) and the local arrest or robbery of the week."

"I like how you talk when you tell me your life," Scarlen whispered to him

"Oh you do. Well, I like talking freely with you about myself, but I need to know?" He paused before finishing. "What are the things that you like?" Allen asked admiring the caramel skin girl.

"What I like?" her words where still slightly above a whisper, "I like you." her Spanish accent floated over her phrases. "I think that you're very nice." she lifted her glass coyly to her lips.

Allen felt a wave of emotions flood over him. Feeling a breeze of love forming, he stared into the street; unsure how to reply to her statement. Trying to gather the strength to look her in the eye; he asked himself, "is this it? Have I had enough time to prepare to for this?" Wanting to say something heartfelt, he stumbled, searching for words. Compassionately, she helped him through the moment.

"My girlfriends thought you were a friend of ours. Someone we already know. That's why we were staring at you."

"Who is he? One of your old boyfriends?" Allen wondered aloud.

"I dated him for a while; but, he was…something like you, but different."

"Like me? How is that? What's his name?" Allen asked.

"Jason, but now that I really look at you. I can see the difference." She shook her head. "I have to go home, to Malmo,"

"I wish I could go to Malmo." Allen replied.

"Why don't you?" She asked.

"All right." Allen held back his enthusiasm well, "but I need to go and pick up my bags back at Fittja. You want to come with me?"

"Yes."

The Life and Times of Allen Court

*

They rode in a comfortable silence. Allen kept repeating in his head the moments before. He hoped everything would keep progressing but reserved his expectations. "I'm going to let this force go freely. In a way, it's good she mentioned her ex. Just reminds me to put the brakes on handing over my heart. If she's something good, I'll do the right thing." He looked over at Scarlen and caught his reflection in her eye.

The subway car came closer to the station. He told Scarlen about his friends Daniel and Keisha, Ashtu and Akili.

"Keisha is real nice. I have my bags over her house. You can meet my other friend Akili. You already met Daniel yesterday."

The train came to a screeching halt, letting them off at an empty station. They walked out together and rode the escalator up. "She's nice, a little bit shy though," thought Allen.

They neared Akili's door. On ringing the bell, Akili answered with a loving welcome.

"My son, come in, come in!"

Allen introduced Scarlen to Akili.

"Welcome." Akili said to Scarlen as she smiled.

"Is Daniel here?" Allen asked Akili.

"Yes." she said in her bursting voice. "He's eating with Keisha. Come, get something to eat."

"You want to eat?" Allen asked Scarlen? Scarlen shook her head slowly.

"Come on, please. You can meet my friends while we are here."

She softly looked at him answering yes.

"Thank You." Allen told her. On entering the hallway, he took off his shoes and slipped on an extra pair of sandals that Akili had especially for guests. Allen took

96

Scarlen's coat and hung it in the closet. They walked into the small kitchen, greeted by Keisha and Daniel. They waited as the food was prepared.

"Brother!" Keisha exclaimed at Allen's entrance.

"How are you Keisha?" Allen asked moving towards her. "This is Scarlen."

Scarlen stood directly behind Allen. "Say hello, Lady." Scarlen smiled shyly. Keisha's voice broke her silence.

"She is pretty. You are welcome here." Keisha told Scarlen, as she moved from behind Allen.

Akili looked on smiling.

Allen introduced everyone to Scarlen. Daniel left his seat and walked over taking Scarlen's hand. Allen told Daniel she was from the Dominican Republic; at that point, they greeted each other in Spanish. Akili insisted they stay to eat. Allen walked over to the table, placing his hand on Scarlen's shoulder, reassuring her with a nod that it was fine. Scarlen sat near him with Daniel across from her. Akili brought over a large pot filled with spaghetti and sauce. The aroma increased his appetite

"Have a beer, son." Akili handed a filled glass to Allen.

"Thank you." Allen motioned to Scarlen, but she declined. Daniel had mixed himself a drink and was having a good time finishing it. Passing the food around the table, everyone started having individual conversations using English as the main language.

Daniel stopped for a moment and spoke with Scarlen asking her questions in Spanish. Allen took notice of how Daniel's tone and inflections changed when he reverted to his mother language. No longer relaxed his tone was more aristocratic as he questioned her.

From the type of conversation they were having, Allen noticed a change in Scarlen's reactions as well. In one instant, she seemed hesitating and in another, beating him to an answer. Allen was more concerned in evaluating the reactions than the direct translation. He determined they were discussing her family in her native country and then contrasted it with living in Sweden.

Allen refocused his attention on the beer and food and was happy that everyone was so open. He ate his food unbeknown that Akili had been watching how Scarlen looked at him.

"You are in love, hugh?" Akili asked Scarlen loudly.

Scarlen blushed and looked into her plate.

"Yes!" Akili said loudly. "She's in love!"

Scarlen only looked on. Daniel came to her rescue and began talking about the places they had visited during the day.

"What did you think of that ship today?" Daniel asked Allen.

"The Vasa? It looked real nice, too bad it sank. The designer didn't take in full consideration the weight of the canons. I'm sure the designer died along with the ship."

"Are you speaking of the Vasa Museum by the harbor?" Keisha asked.

"Yes, we went there earlier in the day." Daniel told her. While they had been talking, Keisha went over to the cupboard and grabbed a tall bottle of Rum. She held the bottle, holding it over Daniel's cup; with his nod, she obliged him. Allen took this as his cue; he asked Keisha for the keys to her apartment, so that he could get his things. She gave him the key, he then excused himself from the table.

"My son, you are going where?" Akili asked him with a sly grin.

"I'm going to Malmo tonight."

"I see, I see. You have fun tonight."

Allen and Scarlen gathered their belongings and left the building as others continued their conversations.

Scarlen broke the silence.

"Your friends are fun."

"Yeah. I think so, they are a little drunk too.'

Scarlen giggled.

"You didn't drink a thing. Why not? You don't drink?"

"Yes. I do." She informed him. "They didn't have *my* drink there."

"*Your* drink?" Allen said sarcastically. "What is your drink?"

"Tequila." Scarlen smiled.

"Tequila? I should have guessed." Allen laughed as he approached Keisha's building.

"This is it." He opened the door for her and watched her small frame glide through the door.

"One moment." Allen turned on the light and lifted up his bag that was near the front door. While rumbling through his clothes, the possibilities of what might happen next began floating through his mind. His feelings of attraction grew stronger.

"Obviously, she must be feeling the same," he thought, "Otherwise, she wouldn't be here. I want to kiss her, but I don't want to get ahead of myself, I've got to do something. " thought Allen.

"Say what's up…" Allen began.

"What's up?" Scarlen teased him.

"You're funny. Got jokes now?" Allen asked, she giggled.

He stepped closer to her and gave her a hug; she let him, "All good so far," he thought and decided to push for more. He leaned in for a kiss, but Scarlen leaned back, with an amused look in her eye. "Oh, you don't want to kiss me, do you?" mused Allen.

Scarlen looked at him showing no response.

"Ughhh... so tell me." Allen was hesitant. "If I go home with you, where will I sleep?" She looked at him curiously.

"I have a bed; and right next to it I have a couch. You can sleep in my bed and I will sleep on the couch."

"Well, that is nice of you to let me sleep in the bed." Allen said. 'Damn! I'm not going to get some tonight.' He thought. 'I had better make the most of it. I've already said I would go. I can't back out now.'

~

They gathered their bags and stepped off the train. The time was near midnight. Scarlen led the way, walking past the station and coming closer to a highway. Watching the night sky, Allen followed her lead. The moon glowed brightly as he found himself in the middle of a large field with her. They continued to walk along in silence. He looked around and noticed that he was nearing a chain linked fence that surrounded a soccer field. Allen wasn't trying to rush the conversation. The mood was one he was growing increasingly comfortable with. Scarlen began to speak.

"Do you want to get a movie?"

"That's cool?"

"We have to go to the store. It's right there." She pointed ahead towards the fence.

"I live near the store."

They walked into a little kiosk. Allen walked over to the video section as Scarlen measured the candy in the different plastic cases.

"Scarlen. What movie do you want?"

She walked over to where Allen was standing and began to look over the titles.

She grabbed one. "Have you seen this?" She asked.

"No, but I want to see it."

She walked over to the counter and paid for the movie.

"Yeah I've wanted to see that movie for a while. Is it in English?"

"Yes." They walked across the street to the apartment building adjacent to the kiosk. After walking up two flights of stairs, Scarlen opened the door to a small studio apartment. He laid his bags down near the front door and walked forward into the apartment. Allen could see a small twin bed directly in front of him; he turned a corner where a giant television stood directly in front of the couch.

"So that's the famous couch you were telling me about?"

Scarlen smiled coyly.

"Want something to…drink?"

"Yeah."

"You can put the movie in." She motioned towards the television. Allen fast forwarded through the promos. She took a shower and came back dressed in sweats and T-shirt. They sat quietly on the couch. Scarlen stared silently at the screen.

"Something tells me I'm not going to feel the same about her after this." Allen was filled with emotions coming from all directions. "What will come after this? Is she the love I've wanted to find here?" The movie played on. Allen glanced at her face; her eyes were fixed on the screen. "What is she thinking? Does she believe the same thing I do?" Allen thought, turned his attention to the movie. Glad that the words were still in English, he tried reading the Swedish subtitles but could only make out a few of the translations. Scarlen grabbed the bag of candy that she had purchased earlier and placed some chocolate inches from Allen's lips. He accepted, feeling her fingertips lightly trace his mouth.

The Life and Times of Allen Court

Allen's thoughts were shifting between the movie and Scarlen. She won out. He raised himself up and before he could stop, began kissing her lightly on the cheek. She turned her mouth toward his and they began kissing slowly. Within the kiss, Scarlen sighed.

"The movie..." Scarlen tried to speak.

"Forget the movie." Allen drew closer.

Thankfully, it was ending.

"If its okay, I'm gonna take a shower." Allen told her.

Scarlen went to her closet, handing Allen a bath towel. He went into the bathroom. He could smell the fragrance that Scarlen had been wearing as he undressed. The water was still warm. He poured his soap on the small towel she had given him and began to scrub his body. "I feel strong." Allen thought and stepped out of the shower to dry off. He placed on his underwear keeping his shirt off. Upon leaving the bathroom, he put his clothes in his bag.

Allen looked to see Scarlen staring at her television screen. Slow music played from the stereo. Sitting down next to her she came closer to him. She wrapped her slender arm around him; he was amazed at the strength of her slim body. Allen softly caressed her breasts and moved down ever so slowly to her waist. She was small, but her body was firmly built. He could feel her hands massaging the muscles along his back. Allen lifted her up and carried her to the bed. Laying her down, he kissed her neck as she ran her fingers through his hair. She positioned herself beneath him and held his head as he slowly moved along her neck. She lifted herself from the bed and pulled off her shirt; exposing a soft, beige bra that blended with her caramel skin. He kissed her breasts, hearing her moan softly. He took his time, moving along her stomach until he reached her panty line. She took her pants down, tossing them to the side.

102

Her body now fully exposed, shown a curvaceous side that was not revealed through her small frame; her g-string underwear matched her bra. Allen started kissing the outline of it. He pulled the remaining pieces of clothing off.

"You are going to enjoy this," he thought as he began kissing her skin. He felt her body shake so he pressed on further. She moaned heavenly, like music. Scarlen pulled Allen upon her and began kissing him intensely. She got on top of him, kissing him from his mouth down to his chest. The favor was being returned to him with equal enthusiasm. Filled with so much passion, Allen took the lead, pulling her back on top of him. Stopping a moment he contemplated where he had placed a condom. He crept out of the bed and grabbed his pants in the hallway. After finding one, he came back to Scarlen before she could cool down. When he reached the bed, she pulled him to her. He kissed her again and let his fingers, and tongue, get her to the point perfect enough to enter. It was evident she was hot when her legs opened wide before him. He raised himself over her and entered her slowly. Upon the moment of penetration, Allen inhaled while Scarlen moaned loudly.

Amidst moans, he pushed himself even harder at her insistence. A stronger sensation began to rise as he gathered momentum. She grinded upon him, matching his thrusts, meeting in the middle. As they moved together, their moans increased.

He tenderly whispered in her ear. 'Your love is so good.' He watched her body rise, as beads of his sweat moistened her breasts. He kissed her mouth, stirred between the feeling and the sight. Hugging her hips with his palms, he gripped her tightly as he moved smoothly within her. In and out, watching, waiting, Scarlen began to shift faster. Allen leaned in whispering in her ear, speaking to her softly. Scarlen moans increased as the

103

tempo changed. They were coming closer to finishing as they both began to push themselves quickened. She told him she was coming, Allen moved faster, no longer holding back. Heat rising, his heart rate increased, her moans coincided with his, in their first moments of release.

*

Scarlen rose in the morning looking as beautiful as sunshine. She gently stroked his chest waking him. In turn, Allen kissed her passionately. They made love for the last time.

"Give me a kiss for everything. I'm gonna see you later." Allen told her.

"Why you have to live in Finland?" She said irritated, making a face. She spoke with thoughtful pauses that were laced in part sex, part casual manner. The woman was a mystery he wanted to know. The morning sun broke through the window.

"Why you have to live in Sweden?" He replied mockingly. They examined each other. Allen shifted his leg over Scarlen's. He took her in his arms laughing as they kissed. Scarlen lifted her right hand and began to caress his face while her left hand rested upon his chest.

"You're heart is beating so fast." She said kissing him on his neck.

"It feels like its going to break" Allen replied torn. Scarlen stretched past his neck and whispered into his ear.

"I want you." Allen was silent. "Are you hungry?" She asked, changing the subject.

He nodded. She went into her kitchen to cook breakfast while Allen showered. His original plan was to go back to Stockholm and prepare to leave the next day for Finland. With the sudden introduction of Scarlen, he debated on staying another day with her before returning to the city.

"You know I want you to come and visit me. Okay."

She nodded.

"I'm serious."

She continued to look at him. "What is this woman thinking?" he thought.

"Come see me in a few weeks." Allen told her.

"I will." she said quieting him.

Allen gathered up his bags and began to walk out the tiny apartment. Scarlen showed him the way to the train station.

"Why you got to live in Finland?" She repeated again, angrily to the road.

"Meet me half way," was Allen's reply. He never imagined meeting a Caribbean beauty in a cold Nordic country. He began to think to himself. His head was racing as he gathered his bags

They reached the train station; while walking to the train platform, the reserved lady lifted her face for a kiss. Allen was surprised; she had been so aloof during the walk to the train.

He kissed her before leaving. "Don't worry. I'll be back." Allen tried to reassure her. For Scarlen, it was no way of telling.

She smiled and waited for the train to pull off. Allen was sad-hearted at leaving Scarlen. He comforted himself with the notion of seeing her again. He took a seat in the middle of the train.

~

The train ride went by quickly; he was lost in thoughts of the night before.

The Life and Times of Allen Court

"I wonder what will come of this." I hope she will take me up on my offer to come. He arrived at the station feeling a desire to rest. He neared the apartment and ran into Akili and Keisha leaving the grocery store. Akili carried a large bag of groceries.

"My son!" Akili bellowed.

"What's up?" Allen grinned, smiling at her enthusiasm. "Hey, what's going on here?" Allen asked.

"We're heading back to Akili's place." Keisha broke in cheerfully. "How are you?"

"I'm good. Here let me take that for you." Allen took the bag from Akili's hands.

"Brother, so did you have fun?" Keisha asked with a mischievous gleam in her eye.

"Yeah, I would have to say it was fun." Allen tried "to play it off" but a smile began to form on his lips, giving him away. He knew what Keisha was interested in.

"Did you bula, bula?" Keisha edged on.

"Bula, bula? Ain't that a song? What's a bula bula?" He asked.

"That means sex in Swahili." Keisha finished for him.

"If that's what it means then, I did a lot of that. Can't wait to get some more either."

Akili and Keisha bent over in laughter.

"How many times. One? Two?" Akili asked, with Keisha leaning in trying to catch the latest gossip. "More."

"Three, was it four." Akili continued. Allen nodded his head, thinking.

"I'd say about that."

"Yes!" Akili let out a breath. "My son is strong!" Akili proudly patted Allen on the back. Allen nodded humbly.

"I never thought about it like that. But thanks."

"You must be tired." Keisha said.

"I feel really good," Allen said as they approached the apartment. "I have to get ready to leave in the morning. I don't want to go, but I have school later. Is Daniel here?"

"He has not arrived back yet!" Keisha exclaimed.

"He knows we have to leave in the morning; so if he is not back tonight I'm sure I'll catch him later on the boat."

Chapter 10
On Thin Ice

Allen sat in the sauna, sweating buckets. The orange heat from the sauna sweat box pressed upon his chest. He wiped sweat away from his forehead. He had not been able to breathe properly since his trip back from Stockholm. With the compression of his nose, plus the intense heat; he felt like his body was locked inside some private war.

Allen took a deep breath forcing his lungs to inhale the hot air. He could feel the phlegm breaking in his chest. He relaxed, realizing that he was breathing without constriction for the first time in two days. "Extreme times, call for extreme measures," he thought breaking away from his initial negative reaction to the steam sauna. The sauna was one of those methods that he had not been willing to try. Daniel had told him that it would help with the cold. "I guess its working." Allen thought as he sat in the sauna with one Finnish man. The man drank two beers within ten minutes; after Allen entered the sauna; the man threw ladles full of water over the blazing rocks causing clouds of steam to fill the room while he drank. The heat wrapped around his chest, for a moment, it made him feel as if he could not bare to stay in the room any longer. The Finnish man cheered himself on in a twisted manner, pointing at the temperature, one hundred and twenty degrees.

Allen wanted to scream at him. But as the sweat dropped off him, and his breathing became smoother, he began to signal to pour more water over the rocks. "This heat might not be so bad." He left the sauna going to the shower, washing off. He returned to the sauna finding the man in the same place, drinking another beer. I had heard the French Connection say they like to go into the sauna before they start drinking.

Walking back to his apartment, Allen was not as cold as before he entered the sauna. "No wonder so many Finnish people have these in their homes. It's a way to deal with the cold winters here. Especially since the days grow increasingly shorter." Allen thought. Nightfall had started coming by three p.m. He had been fore-warned by Saga, that soon, they would be seeing only three to four hours of daylight in the next couple of weeks. "It's a wrap. From now on, the sauna is my thing. I need to keep that internal heat going," he thought, turning the key to his door.

*

Within the last couple of months, Allen had been through a lot. Traveling to different countries and meeting new people everyday he began to evaluate how this would affect his future.

"I wonder how this thing with me and Scarlen is going to play out." He had talked with her on the phone and made arrangements to see her in another week. "There are still feelings I have for Cynthia I haven't dealt with, he thought to himself realistically. "I don't know how this is going to work. Saga has become a good friend and I am not about to mess that up. I don't need the guilt of breaking her heart. Zaleha has fallen through the cracks and I don't care, this juggling hearts is beginning to wrack my brain and tire me out."

Allen looked at his calendar, "This weekend; I will be back with Scarlen. I haven't written Cynthia yet; I need to make a move, either a step forward or stay friends. Truthfully, that means I have to give up Scarlen and I don't want to. Not at this point, it's all too early to say. For once, I am glad that I have time on my side. I know I can be better than what I have been; I just need to make up my mind. Cynthia is still in my heart, maybe this time. I'll see what I have to do…," he paused. "To choose." He stared at the calendar shaking the thoughts. "Let me get ready for class."

~

"I don't know how to ice skate. If I get out here on this ice, I might get hurt but I got to learn one way or another." Allen thought, pushing himself onto the skating rink. He had been use to "playing the star" when it came to the Finnish sports, having the advantage of playing games similar to the ones back home. "Now here's something new!" Allen looked around; everyone else was having an easy time while the smallest steps were having him fall flat on his face. He fell nearly twenty times before being able to glide on the ice for more than thirty seconds. Kru, the instructor tried to tell him to stop but he wouldn't listen. Allen continued on pushing himself through his pain. He circled his way around the rink, one time without falling before sitting upon the bleachers. His legs had given out on him. He had twisted his right ankle early and now the left knee began to swell up with fluid. His twenty minute walk back to

Kortehlia took nearly an hour. "This is going to cause problems with my trip to see Scarlen this weekend," He thought.

*

Scarlen put down the phone.

"So he says he cannot come because of a bruised leg? Is it a lie? I don't know what to believe? My friends have warned me to be careful about dating foreigners. Yes, they are fun, yes, they are a good time, but no, they cannot stay."

"I was hoping that this one would be cut from a different mold but it's happening again. He is too much like Jason. I was hoping he was different. My last relationship with a traveler ended up with me facing months of heartache. Not again," she told herself. "I'm going to cut this one off before it goes any further." She busied herself by calling up her friends. "I'm not going to wait by the phone any longer," she thought dialing up her friend Kayla.

"Are you going out this weekend? If you are, I'm coming too."

~

Allen lay in bed for two days icing his knee. Scarlen had not called him since the day he told her about the ice-skating incident. Saga had dropped by bringing him some food speaking for a moment then leaving angrily. He sat in bed trying to decipher what in the conversation that caused her to react the way she did. All of a sudden it began to hit him like a sack of bricks. He was rumbling off his confusion between his choice of Scarlen and Cynthia. When speaking about how meeting

Scarlen had been making him see things different, Saga screamed out to him.

"You are so selfish!" She yelled. "What about me…" Allen looked at her for a moment but before he could factor it all in, she changed her sentence. "I mean Cynthia." She stated.

"I don't know how to respond?" He said.

"That's not good enough," she snapped.

"It has to be for now." Saga stared at him.

"Look, Cynthia ain't really thinking about me. She's out doing her thing; and me and you…" a feeling of guilt began to creep into him but he shook it off. .."I just have to do what's best for me."

"Yeah." Saga stood looking at him angrily. "You keep on doing what's best for *you*." Saga mimicked him. And for *me*, I'm not going to listen to anymore of this." Saga stormed out the room.

"Man, can't win for losing. Now I got three women mad at me and I can't do nothing about it. I'm going from top dog to the dog house in a matter of days. I told Saga not to get into me. I care for Cynthia but she ain't around. And now?" Allen paused for a moment.

"I'm starting to think that what I wanted to build with Scarlen is going to fall to the wayside," Allen thought. He had called twice, but no one picked up. A far cry from when they were speaking daily. "Not much else to do, but wait."

He busied himself by picking up a book. Raheem stopped by.

"What's up, Allen?" he said, "Looks, like you been laid, out."

"It's only temporary." I was reading over this book that was talking about how different types of building architecture came about." Allen looked outside at the buildings out his window. "This type of project housing came about in the nineteen twenty's due to the black exodus from the southern states to the North."

"What do you mean?" Raheem asked.

"During the nineteen twenties to the forties, Black people were leaving the Southern states by the tens of thousands, going into the more industrial North for work. At the time, cities were flooded with new people day in and day out. They needed some way to house all the newly arrived people. Social scientist had an idea that they could stack poor upon poor, through the advent of tenement buildings.What we call, 'Projects.' This idea was first started in Chicago, with its buildings."

"Building the first modern-day ghetto's." Raheem interjected.

"The idea worked so well, it went across the United States; and eventually, the world."

"So, it's true, what they say. The world is a ghetto."

"A ghetto use to be any place where one type of ethnic group would live, like all Polish ghettos or all Swedish ghettos. If you say ghetto now, people automatically think black neighborhood. But ghetto, originally is any poor neighborhood. I seen them in many of the countries I've traveled."

"It's a part of life that we have to deal with. Some people are going to have more and most people less." Raheem finished. "Yo, what's up with that Swedish trip you were on?"

"It may be a done deal. I should be there, today, if it wasn't for me falling on that ice. I may have to chalk it up to experience." The doorbell rang. "Can you get that for me?" Raheem opened the door. It was Kane.

"I heard about your accident are you okay?" Kane asked concerned.

"Yeah. I am doing better. What's going on with you?"

112

"Same thing as usual, classes and traveling. You know there's a travel special for two hundred dollars round trip to one of five different cities. I'm thinking Prague. You want to go? I'm leaving next week."

"This is kind of last minute; but yeah, I think I could make it if my leg heals. Next week we have the whole week out. I'll tell you something for sure tomorrow." Allen stood up.

His leg forced him to hobble around. "Damn, I don't know if physically I'll be able to go anywhere."

*

"Did you make up your mind yet about taking a trip to Prague?" Kane asked as he saw Allen walking down the street four days after seeing him in his apartment.

"I'm not going to be able to do it." Allen told him. The money he had was starting to run low. "The most meaningful trip would be back to Scarlen," he thought. Daniel rode a bicycle up alongside him. "I may go back to Stockholm, a little later then expected to see what's good."

"How are you by the way?" Daniel asked. "Your injury is it getting better?"

"Yeah, its fine." Allen said. Kane spoke next.

"Your Stockholm trip. Was it good?" Allen nodded. Kane went on talking to Daniel. "You know, I hear the ladies treat him like he was famous."

"I don't know about all of that. But, I been having a good time." Allen finished. "Met a little, lovely, young tender; she was sweet on me for a while, but it's kind of panning out. I'll give it one more shot this weekend."

"Those things happen. Sorry to hear you're not going to be able to go."

"It's cool. I really wanted to be able to say, 'caught a flight to Prague reading Soul on Ice, drinking 'yac' with my friends, I never felt so nice.' But you know, maybe on the next rip." Kane shook his head at Allen's' statement, then, held out his hand. Allen gave his a hand clap. "I'm going to Stockholm this weekend. See you later."

Kane watched him walk off; then nodded, goodbye.

~

Akili had said that the Tanzanian party would be fun. Music blared over the speakers in a large dining hall area. Rows of circular tables aligned the northern side of the hall. A small dj booth was perpendicular south. Along the side was a buffet with various African style food. In the middle of the surroundings was an open dance floor.

Allen sat along with Akili and waited for Keisha to arrive. He sat watching people dance. Akili went to the dance floor finding a partner. Their bodies moved to the strong rhythms that came from the speakers. Allen wanted to relax but felt tense. He had called Scarlen with no answer. "What's going on?" He replayed the cruise the day before over.

The boat ride had gone smoothly. He had told Akili and Keisha that he wanted to see them first before meeting with Scarlen. On the boat, Allen spoke with Scarlen briefly; she gave him a weak reassurance that things were okay between them.

"The next few days would be the real test," he thought as two shapely, Tanzanian women looked at him flirtatiously. The tight red dresses clung to their breast and hips. "If I wasn't aiming for Scarlen, I would be trying to do something with them."

The thought raised a level of doubt in his mind. "Am I even with her? She had been acting strange lately." The music began to shift as he sat at the table deep in thought. Akili walked back to the table and handed Allen a small plate of chicken, salad, and vegetables. He thanked her, doing his best to rid the doubt from his mind. Keisha walked in. Spotting Allen, she nearly sprinted over to him, planting a kiss upon his cheek.

"Brother how've you been?" she said excitedly as she gave him a hug.

"I've been good. I arrived last night."

"My, my, my." Keisha shook her head in disbelief. "You sure move around."

A light skinned man stepped to the side of Keisha and upon making eye contact with her they spoke as if they were long lost family reunited. Keisha introduced the man as Samuel. Allen shook his hand making the regular introductions. Samuel held the widest smile on his face as he continued spoke with Keisha. He took a seat next to Allen.

"Brother." Samuel said enthusiastically.

"Peace. How are you?"

"Fine. Are you enjoying yourself here?" Samuel asked.

"So far, everything has been good." Allen told him. "I really like how friendly people are here. Especially, my sisters over here." Samuel shook his head in agreement.

"It's no problem. I will have to say I'm sorry that our ancestors were so separated that we let so many of you get taken away."

"Taken away?" Allen started to realize where he was going with his statement.

"I'm ashamed. We should have come for you. Do you know the total population of Africa is estimated at?" Samuel asked him.

"About seven hundred eighty, to eight hundred million." Allen estimated.

"Correct. Do you know how much it's estimated to be if the slave trade hadn't changed it?"

"About a billion and a quarter, more or less. But now you have the HIV/AIDS epidemic ripping through countries like the plague." Samuel nodded.

"It's attacking the vital power of the youth. The energy we need to survive and continue."

Allen was impressed by the seriousness, yet, friendly manner of Samuel. He looked a few years older than he; but through these few moments of conversation, he could tell that his mind was mature.

"How old are you?" Allen asked as Samuel waved to a passing couple.

"I'm twenty six."

"Do you have any children?" Allen asked as Samuel's' grin widened.

"My wife is seven months pregnant," he responded proudly.

"Do you want a boy or girl?"

"It doesn't matter, "God gave this life to me!""

"That's beautiful." Allen said, smiling himself. Keisha came over to the table holding a drink for Allen. He took a sip, happy that he came to the party. One can always find true happiness if one knows true appreciation. Akili was speaking to a man in a gray suit. He was stocky; dark skinned and had a medium cropped Afro. She waved Allen over to her. He walked to the introduced him as Dr. Panula, a physician that worked in the Tanzanian government before coming to Sweden. Allen shook his hand.

"I hear from Akili, that you travel often. Are you making any plans to go to Tanzania?" He asked Allen as they stood up watching the crowd dance.

"After meeting with Akili and coming here, I've made it a point to one day visit." The man smiled warmly toward the crowd. "I'm glad that you're enjoying yourself here. I came to this country nearly ten years ago. It's a good country, but I go back and forth to help my people in my homeland. We have so many issues to be addressed; but we don't lose heart," Dr.Panula told him. "As long as we are dealing with facts, we can never lose."

He shook Allen's hand. "One day if you can go to my country, you'll be welcomed there." Dr. Panula excused himself and walked over to speak with a couple who motioned towards him. Allen now stood near a hallway. An attractive, caramel-skinned woman caught his eye. She looked shyly at him. Her hair was thinly braided, hanging to the middle of her back. Allen took one step in her direction when he felt a hand touch him over his shoulder. He turned to see a middle-aged Swedish woman. Her short, red hair and black rimmed glasses made her look like a school teacher to him.

"My name is Mirra." The woman said holding out her hand. Allen not wanting to be rude, shook her hand saying his name.

"I'm Allen could you…" he turned to look at the girl was but she had walked out of sight. The woman still held his hand. He returned to his attention to her. She relaxed her grip and released his hand.

"Excuse me, but I had to say hello to you. I see that you haven't danced tonight?"

"I haven't felt much like dancing."

"You don't want to dance with me?" She asked seductively. Allen's silent look informed her that she had missed her target. "What is it? You have a girlfriend?"

"I have a woman I'm seeing." She nodded.

117

"If you change your mind, I'll be here."

Allen walked back to the table to sit with Akili.

"My son, I see you with that Swedish woman. Are you thinking of a new love?" Akili asked sarcastically. Allen shook his head. She grabbed his hand.

"Come, let's dance."

This time he did not refuse. He walked with Akili to the middle of the dance floor. Keisha moved about with Samuel at her side. Allen began moving with them matching their steps. Akili yelled loudly, startled at how quickly Allen adapted to the changing rhythms.

"Look he's doing it." Akili said as Allen danced with Keisha. "Of course he can, he is our brother." Keisha said in recognition. Allen looked to see the girl with the braided hair, dancing near him. He moved in front of her. She looked him in the eyes, and then smiled.

"It's all good," he thought as the music played on.

They danced for two more songs before the DJ announced it was closing time. People began walking out and gathering their coats at the door. Before he could ask her name, her friend pulled her away.

"What was that?" Allen thought and laughed it off. "I'm going to see my lady tomorrow that should be the only thing on my mind." He walked over to the coat check meeting the Swedish woman again. She wrote on a small piece of paper and handed the note to Allen.

Allen looked to see her number and a small message, *if you change your mind*. The girl in the red dress with braided hair walked by with her friend. Allen looked up just in time to see her walk out with her motioning for him to come towards her.

"I'm going to leave this alone." Allen looked at the woman nodding a silent goodbye. Akili walked out with her friends with Keisha not far behind. "I'm not changing my mind after coming this far. Win or lose."

"I'll pay for the taxi, let's go back." Allen told them. Keisha wanted to party some more but Akili wanted to sleep. Keisha said she would meet them tomorrow getting in a cab solo.

Allen hailed a cab opening the door for Akili. He slid inside the back seat.

"I had a good time tonight." Akili told her.

"Yes, me too." Akili agreed. "But I can see on your face you are thinking of that woman. I am telling you now don't worry. If she's yours, she will be there for you. If not, then she is a silly thing." Allen liked her comforting words.

"Thank you." he said to her; before turning to the window slowing his thoughts. "I wonder if she is mine."

*

Allen woke with a note on the table. Akili had gone to work earlier and didn't want to wake him. She wrote that she had some food for him in the microwave. He looked at the time and noticed that it was fast approaching twelve.

"How long did we stay out? I'm up now let me call Scarlen." Allen felt apprehensive about the phone call. "What if I don't get her? Or worse yet, she doesn't want to talk with me. I've changed my whole vibe for this girl; don't turn your back on me now." He dialed the number getting no response for the first four rings. Someone picked up.

"Scarlen?" Allen asked.

"No, this is Kayla."

"Is Scarlen there?" Allen asked confused. "I thought she would be in by now."

"She went out in the morning." Kayla told him. "I don't know when she will be back."   "What is going

119

on," he thought? "It's starting to look like it's going to be my turn to lose."

"She knows that I am here and I only have a few days to spend with her." Allen spat out. "Let me get this out in the open, does she want to see me?"

"You have to speak to her about that." Kayla started to sound like an angry mediator.

"By the time I speak with her, it will be time for me to go." Allen said in recognition of what was happening.

"Maybe you should just come here." She told him.

"You know what? I may do that! Can you meet me at the train station? I don't know how to get to the apartment from the railway."

"Yes, I can. But you have to tell me what time you are leaving so I can meet you."

"I'll come on the five o'clock train. I'll call you first just to make sure that you are there. Is that cool?"

"That's fine." The way Kayla responded, Allen had no clue to her thoughts, but was grateful for her help.

"Thank you." He told her.

"I'll see you later, Allen." With that, she hung up the telephone. "Finally, getting somewhere," he thought. "I got to see what happens."

~

"Before buying this ticket, I better call Kayla first." Allen walked through the busy railway station towards a phone booth. Swarms of people were coming and going through the brightly colored station. There was a major subway connection directly across from it. Everywhere he looked, Allen saw backpackers. Groups of students were holding conversations while they waited for friends to arrive. Allen put his phone card into the slot holder. He dialed the number with no one picking up. "Pick up, pick up!"

"Hey." He heard over the phone he thought it might have been Scarlen but for some reason he asked for Kayla.

"Hello, is Kayla there." Silence. "It's Scarlen," he thought but she said nothing.

"Scarlen, it's Allen." Still a pause, then suddenly he heard a dial tone. She hung up the phone.

"What! I can't believe it! I got my answer." Allen stood at the phone, shaking his head in disbelief. Groups of people walked by laughing and talking as the world moved in slow motion for him. He stumbled backwards trying to make sense of his situation. "Wait! I'll call again." He dialed the number this time no one picked up at all. He shook his head sadly. A man in a nearby telephone booth noticed the disturbed look on his face.

"What's wrong?" The man asked curiously. Allen looked at him in a daze of confusion.

"I don't know?" He walked backwards not wanting to explain his loss to a stranger. "I should have seen this for what it was. Not what I wanted it to be. She could have told me before I came back." He began to walk to the subway platform to make his way back to Fittja. Thoughts flooded his head as he walked through the station. "If I had known this, I would have stayed home. She could at least be woman enough to talk with me instead of hanging up the phone! If I had taken the train up there to see her, then, what would she have done? She probably would have let me wait at the train station, alone; after I came all this way to see her."

The thought infuriated him. Allen whirled around and headed back to the phone booth. He angrily dialed Scarlen's number with no idea what he was going to say as the phone rang. The answering machine picked up. He heard the American music in the background with her speaking over it in Swedish. "Yeah, that's right," he thought as he listened to the intro, "life gives you no guarantees." He hung up the phone.

*

While riding back to Fittja in the subway car, Allen looked at the wall; his thoughts drifted back to what Cynthia had told him the last time they met face to face.

"You are trapped by your materialism, your good time."

"What do you mean? I'm not materialistic."

"Maybe, but you're always looking for your good time. Unsatisfied with your reality; the in between highs causes you to suffer, turning your good times into a trap."

"I don't know how much time I have. I just feel I have to use everything I have before it's gone. You know. Before, I lose it."

"It's never going to be gone; what you need to lose is that way of thinking." And with that said, she leaned over and kissed him. Allen had to hold back a smile upon remembering the moment. "One lady pulls me down, another pulls me up. I need to keep it real with the one who has always been on my side. I'm finally starting to realize this."

~

He tried to justify his call back to Scarlen but could not. By the time he arrived back to Fittja, he wondered how he to rationalize the story to Akili. He knocked on her door to be greeted by a surprised Akili.

"My son! I thought you would be with Malmo."

"I thought I would be with Malmo too!" Allen said sadly. Akili looked at him warmly. "Well, come in. What happened?" Allen came into the apartment and walked into the kitchen, seeing Keisha. She exchanged a look of surprise as well.

"What happened to your girlfriend?" Keisha asked surprised. "No bula, bula tonight."

"No, nothing for me at all." He repeated, teeth grinding. He explained to them what happened. Embarrassed by what went down and the way he reacted he simply repeated what happened. His pride was hurt from being turned down by a woman he looked to for love.

"Does it have to be like this?" He thought. "Try to find something real and it's just more confusion." His eyes dropped to the floor. Akili put her arm around him rubbing his back.

"It's okay my son. She is young and doesn't understand. You're a good man. So don't you ever hold your head down!" Allen began to laugh wanting to change the subject.

"You look like you're going out."

"Yes. We're going to the bar in the town center, then Savannah's. You must come." Keisha said to him. Allen looked away.

"I don't know if I'm in the mood for all of that tonight."

"Come now, you cannot stay and be sad." Akili told him.

"I can't go like this." Allen held his hands out. Let me shower and change clothes. You can go ahead and I'll meet you up at the center in an hour and half. I'll walk you to the train." He left with them heading to the station. They approached the platform. Three girls passed them up, waving to Allen. Akili laughed out loud.

"See, you don't have to worry about her." She laughed causing Allen to smile.

"Hanging out with you could make a humble mans' head swell." Keisha looked at the girls. "They are still waving to you Allen. You can forget about Malmo and start thinking, Fittja."

"You have all the jokes today." Allen said looking back at the girls. They were in front of the station booth. "Let's meet up in front of the bar in an hour or so. If I don't see you there, I'll just go to Savannah's." He kissed Akili on her cheek.

"It's no problem." She said as the train approached. Allen hugged Keisha. She turned and went down the platform hurrying for the train. Allen went back to the apartment. He looked for signs of the girls but saw no one upon reaching the building. Raheem was coming into Stockholm the next day, to go back to Finland. Raheem had beeen visiting a friend in Gotenburg, Stockholm. Allen shuffled through his bags, looking for Raheem's cell phone number. He dialed getting Raheem on the first ring.

"What's up, dog? It's Allen. I'm in Stockholm now"

"Hey, how are you enjoying yourself?"

"It's all right. And you?"

"Love it! Man, the girls here look so good. And they're *friendly*." Raheem's accent on friendly; let him know that he was getting along well with the women.

"How are you and your girl doing?" Allen did not know want to go into the whole story now.

"You know, "Carpe Diem.""

"Yeah, "Seize the Day."" Raheem said suddenly.

"I should have stayed in bed."

"I get it." He said with nothing more. "I'm coming into town at six. My train is the Gotenburg line four. Meet me at the station."

"That's cool. See you then. Peace." He looked at the time and noticed that he only had an hour left to meet his friends.

Meshawn Deberry

*

Allen stood in front of Savannah's. Allen had gone to the bar walking in and finding no one. Allen walked in Savannah's, to discover the same thing, it was nearly empty. The opposite from the first time he had visited. The feeling was no longer the same. The newness was gone.

The door man of the club had let him walk around to see if his friends were there; but he saw no one. Not wanting to sit in an empty club he waited in front of the building. Hating the cold weather, he tried to keep Scarlen out of his mind. A short blond-haired man with a large black down-goose coat stood near the entrance. The short man put a cigarette to his mouth then patted his pockets for a lighter finding none. He walked over to Allen.

"Excuse me, do you have a light?"

"I don't smoke." Allen told him. From his accent he knew the man was from the US. "Where are you from?" he asked him.

"California."

"It's good to meet someone from home. I'm from the U.S. too; I'm in this study abroad program in Finland."

"How did you get here?" He patted his coat finding a lighter.

"I had a girl here. But…when I came over, she dropped me. Didn't want to get together."

"You too! Can you tell me what the hell is wrong with the women here? One minute they are in love with you; the next, not answering phone calls." The man said agitated.

"I don't know? I am still learning."

"How old are you?' The man asked sternly

"Twenty-one." He looked Allen up and down.

The Life and Times of Allen Court

"Listen. I'm forty eight years old. I tell you, I'm still learning myself and it's never going to end."

"It's crazy to me that the one you want to try to have something with is the same one who wants to play games." Allen said.

"What you want will always pass you by. I had a beautiful Eritrean woman until a week ago. She was telling me how much she loved and cared for me; and then suddenly, she is with another man. Worse yet, he lives across the street from me. I can see them together."

"Damn, that's cold." Allen said. A tall bouncer from the club came over signaling them to either enter or leave. Allen took it as a sign to go.

"Let's walk up the bridge." Allen headed towards a small breezeway. The man walked with him. "Even though my relationship didn't work out, I still say it's a very nice country. Could be good for business too." Allen told the man.

"Some parts of it are good, but they will put a limit on how far you will go." The man told him. "One, because you're black, and the other because you're American."

"It's strange to hear a white guy just tell the truth like that. Usually you guys try to beat around the bush." Allen told him.

"There is a limit to how far *I* can go, as an American here. That is just how it is. The system here will tax your success." They stood over the middle of the bridge. Looking over the water, he could see a small gray mist rising below them. He looked up to see edges of the city perched above him with thousands of glittering lighted windows.

"Beautiful city." Allen spoke aloud caught up in the sight. They began to descend to the other side of the bridge. Up ahead, he could see a busy block with rows of people standing outside waiting to get into clubs. Allen passed one club and got in line for another one. "Might as well do something here."

"I think I'll go in here." Allen told the man.

"I hope that things work out between you and your lady. If you guys are going to try again, it will come down to forgiveness; otherwise, you will only end up hating her when she does make up her mind." Allen told him.

"Thanks for the advice. I hope things pick up for you." Allen nodded the man turned and walked away.

"I'm not about to become some broken old man over a relationship. I guess this shows me who the real choice was. If Cynthia would still like to see me?" Allen turned around. A man approached out of the shadows. Allen looked at him, an instantly could tell he was from the United States. The tall black man was dressed similar to him. He stared directly at Allen.

"Peace. What's up, brother?" The man approached him saying.

"Peace. What's up with you?"

"Nothing for real. I caught the tail end of your conversation. Some girl left your nose wide open?" the man chuckled. "What can you do? Romances that happen fast usually end just as fast." Allen could not figure the man out. "I'm sure it's not the first or last time, either."

"What do you mean?" Allen asked.

"You haven't figured out the game, yet? Some women can be fickle. Say they care about you, then, won't even return your calls, jump from one dude, to the next. Seen it all day, everyday. I can tell, you don't know the game here; but, you might get it right with a little time."

Allen was about to respond angrily but thought about it.

"I guess it wasn't meant to be."

"Don't tell me you one of them? You believe in that meant to be, not meant to be stuff? It is a choice. Maybe for the right reason, maybe for the wrong one? In the end, a decision was made and now, *you,* have to deal with it." Allen looked at him, this time angrily.

"Who are you supposed to be? Black, Mr. Miyagi? What do you know about my situation?"

The man laughed.

"Nothing, directly, but trust, I been through it. More than likely I responded similar to you, just now, when someone tried to enlighten me. Look at it like this. So you lost. Damn, but, it won't be the last time someone pulls one on you. Chalk it up to experience. Once it's all said and done. Are you going to let it mess up your focus? Are you just going to stay mad?"

Allen could feel the adrenaline rise up in him.

"Damn, this cat just met me a second ago, but he is reading my intentions easily. There might be something to what he's saying if I'm that open." The man began to talk again.

"If you're mad, good! Do something about it but make sure it's well thought out. Or you can do one other thing."

"What's that? Let it go?" Allen finished for him.

"Getting smarter already."

Allen shook the response off. The man did not let up.

"You, like most people, can be your own worst enemy. Most of us at one point or another, we tend to get in our own way. Sometimes it's simply by holding on to other peoples nonsense; whether its passion, love, lust or pain."

"Like, what you're trying to do with me."

"Well, yes and no. In the end, it's for you to figure out if it's real, or just some make believe. What I do know, is if you keep crying about the one who did you so wrong, another one, possibly the real one, is slipping away. Just ask yourself this question. Are you going to be just another blind pair of eyes, staring, directly into the sun; who, will never see the light?" The man looked at his watch. "I have to meet someone in a few minutes. Maybe, I'll see you around? We can talk then. One." The man began to walk away.

"Wait!" Allen wanted to speak with him some more but had nothing to say. He blurted out the first thing that came to his mind. "How old are you?" He turned around.

"If it matters, twenty-nine."

"And, you're name?"

"Night. Jason Night." The man walked away throwing up the deuces. Returning into the shadows; nearly, as fast as he came.

"That was strange." Allen thought trying to reason if he had been given a gift or a burden. He headed for the train station that would take him back to Fittja. "I need to look at what I've been doing. Wait a minute! What? Jason? Scarlen? It can't be?" He shook his head. "I'm wasting my time, throwing rocks at the moon. You two can have each other. It's time for me to get right."

~

"I was just here yesterday." Allen walked through the train station waiting for Raheem. He stared at the phone booth from the day before. "I think I had better move on." Allen had booked a ticket on the Silja Line cruise ship earlier that day. The television monitors reported the departing and arrival times for the trains. The Gotenburg arrivals where at four different gates; Raheem, would be at gate number four.

Allen walked around looking for a gate four sign, but couldn't find one. "I don't want to miss him today."

He continued to walk around the station. "I may have to ask someone. The gate was not as packed as it was the day before." He looked to see a tall, young girl leaning in the middle of a column in front of him, she's mixed," he thought. "What do they say here? Half caste." The girl was dressed in a hip-hop fashion. She bobbed her head to the music from her walkman. "No, not again, she is too pretty. I can't keep doing this." He thought. "Something might jump off. I better ask someone else." He turned and looked to his right then to the left and couldn't find the right fit, deciding there wasn't enough time to be choosy; Allen approached the girl.

"Excuse me." Allen said to the girl. She pulled her headphones off as if expecting him to come next to her. She looked at him with deep green eyes and smiled.

"Excuse me." Allen repeated, startled by the softness of her eyes. "I need to find the Gotenburg Exit Number four. I'm waiting for a friend of mine to come."

"You're in the right place." The girl said without a Swedish accent. "I'm waiting for a friend too." The girl continued smiling at him.

"It's about to happen." Allen thought.

"Are you from the states?" Allen asked saying states instead of U.S. "I'm starting to speak English like the foreigners," he thought.

"My father is a Black American, my mother is Swedish. I was born here, but I have gone to school in Michigan to spend some time with my family. What about you?"

"I'm from the Mid-West. I've been doing some traveling in and out of different countries. I was going to school in Finland. Tomorrrow I'm taking a cruise to Helsinki." Her eyes widened.

"You are?" She asked in amazement. "I'm going there tomorrow to see a ballet with my dance troupe."

"Really? And what line are you taking."

"Silja." She responded quickly.

"So, I'll see you tomorrow at six." Allen said knowing the only boat leaving tomorrow was at that time.

"You *are* going!" she said after realizing what he said was true. "Then I guess you will. For a moment, I thought you may have been lying." She looked at him, tensing her eyes. "I know how you American guys are."

"And what way is that?" Allen asked, already knowing what to expect.

"You're players."

"Here we go again," Allen thought as the girl continued.

"I had an American boyfriend when I went to school there. The girls there are all so…" She looked for the word beginning her sentence again. "You know how girls here, dress? Real short skirts, tight tops," She asked.

"Yeah, I know." Allen laughed, reminiscing on the short skirts he viewed the first time he came to Sweden. "I don't mind."

"Well, a lot of the girls there did. They didn't like me much."

"I'm starting to like you a lot." Allen thought. A large group of people began to walk by signaling that a train had arrived.

"We've been talking all this time and haven't even introduced ourselves." Allen said extending his hand.

"Allen."

"Cherie."

"Like the song?"

"It's what I was named after." Allen nodded.

"Are you in school? What do you do?" he asked.

"I'm a dancer. I study dance at the university here in Stockholm. The girl I'm waiting for goes to my school. We break dance together."

"I'd like to see that."

131

"You will if you're on the boat tomorrow." She said confidently.

"Cherie!" A black haired girl wearing a dark blue jacket and matching baggy, dark blue pants and white Adidas shoes came behind her. Cherie turned and opened her arms to her as soon as she recognized the girl's face.

"Emily." Cherie screamed. They embraced each other. Cherie introduced her. "Emily, this is Allen."

They shook hands.

"Emily is cute," he thought. "The ride back is looking better."

"We have to get back. We might go out tonight, if we do, you want to come?" asked Cherie.

"Yeah, I wasn't planning on doing anything," replied Allen.

"What's your number?" She asked him, lifting his spirits. He found a piece of paper to write on.

"I'm staying with friends, but you can call anytime." He wrote down Akili's phone number, handing the paper to her.

"Okay, I'll give you a call later tonight."

"Bye, Cherie." Allen extended his hand.

"Bye, Allen." Cherie said taking his hand, leaned towards him and kissed him lightly on the cheek. "See you tomorrow, "She said walking off with Emily.

"What a turn of events. That was completely unexpected. Now, Raheem where are you? Emily would've been a nice catch." He turned and waited for another ten minutes before spotting him. "Raheem!" Allen shouted towards him.

"I'm running into you all over the world." Allen said to him.

"It's just like we said. It was only going to be a matter of time." Raheem said to him. "I'm taking the

Silja line back to Turku tonight. You want to come with me."

"Yeah, I can go. I need to find out how to get there anyway." They headed for the subway. On the train, Allen told him about meeting Cherie.

"And tomorrow we're going to be taking the same boat together. Who knows, I might be bouncing back from Scarlen already."

"Of course." Raheem said, as he looked up. "This is the stop." They left the train station. The ground was wet with snow. They walked out of the station into a quiet, residential neighborhood. Raheem walked along a small brick pathway.

"So how was it in Gotenburg?" Allen asked as they left the residential section and walked over a highway overpass. The ships were in the distance.

"The girls there are off the chain. I hooked up with a college girl over there, red hair, tight body; now I see why you like it here so much. I'm making plans to come back in a month." Allen looked over to see the port they were heading for.

"All right, one."

"Peace."

Raheem made his way to the dock. Allen turned to walk back to the subway station. The snow was falling heavier now, covering the trees that lined the streets. He reached Akili's apartment a hour later.

"A girl just called for you, I thought it was Malmo; but she said her name was 'Cherie.' I think it was Malmo pretending to be some other girl." Akili said agreeing with her own detective logic.

"Actually, it *is* a girl named Cherie. I just met her in town earlier. We're going to be on the same boat back to Finland tomorrow." He explained to them. Keisha laughed. "You may get some bulla, bula after all."

"Trust, bula, bula is not on my brain right now. I got to get my head together for my trip home; plus, I still miss Scarlen." Akili shook her head.

"If you ask me, I think Malmo is crazy. You'll be okay. I must get some sleep. Goodnight." Akili told him.

"Excuse me, can I use the phone to call Cherie back." Akili handed him her phone.

"Goodnight." Keisha headed for the door stopping for a moment to address Allen. "My brother, this may be goodbye. I know I'll see you again; so, be safe while you're traveling. Goodbye."

"I'll write you when I make it back home. Bye." Allen hugged her one last time; then, she went out the door

Chapter 11
Saying Goodbye

Allen never made the call. He took the girls number but left it at the station. 'There's nothing wrong with her but I need to start living the life that I want to live, today. If I am going to be real with Cynthia I have to stay focused whether she is in front of me or not.'

*

Allen arrived back in Jyvaskyla, twenty minutes ahead of schedule. He waited for the bus to take him back into town. On his arrival, he caught a cab back to Emmannatie. He jumped out of the cab, carrying his bags on his back and trotted up the walkway to his building. On the way he saw Julien approach.

"Julien!" he shouted. Julien jogged closer to him, closing the distance.

"What's up? How was your trip?"

"It was good. Real good." Allen looked up to see the sun setting; a purple mist hanging over the green trees that stood behind his building. Admiring the beauty in the moment, it felt good to be home.

"What!" He paused for a moment. "I just said "home" to here?" He thought shaking his head. Julien glanced at him curiously.

"You look different." Julien squinted his eyes to examine him. "Really? You look …older." Allen thought about his words.

"You know what, I feel older. It's like right now I'm talking to you; but I'm still breaking down all the experience I had and things I have seen in the last few days. I feel like two months have passed, and it's only been a few days." They walked near the door.

"Right now, I'm just glad to be back here. How has everything been going since I've been gone."

"Well, you know that half of the Bounce crew left for St. Petersburg last Tuesday."

"Yeah, that's right! When will they be back?" Allen said remembering.

"December 8th." Julien told him. "That means Daniel won't be back until then," Allen thought.

"That's cool." He said nonchalantly. The elevator opened and climbed to the fourth floor. "I'll see you later." He told Julien leaving.

"Allen, I still want to get those CD's from you." Julien shouted, holding the doors open.

"Yeah, I'll call you later in the week about that."

~

Allen walked into his room and relaxed by slowly, leaning back on his bed. He flipped through his CD case finding a new favorite CD. Listening to music for a moment he decided it was time to make an important phone call. "I'm glad to be back." He picked up the phone and dialed Cynthia's number.

"Hello?" Cynthia picked up.

"Hey, it's Allen. Did you miss me?"

"Yes." He could hear it in her voice.

"I just came back from Stockholm it was real nice. You know, school will be out soon. We had talked before of me coming to visit you. I was wondering is it still okay?"

"Yes it is. When are you going to come?" She quickly responded.

"I can leave after taking my tests, about three weeks or so. I'll let you know for sure by email. You know? Get my thoughts together. Is that fine?"

"That's good! I did miss you while you were away. I have so many things I would like to show you. I wondered if you would call me."

"Really? I've missed you, too. Right now I need to get some rest; I'm just getting in. I'll be in touch later. I'll see you soon. Goodbye."

"Bye."

"That went good. I got to figure out how to get the money to go see her? I have to leave a lot of what I have behind. I may be able to sell the TV and stereo I had bought earlier. Then what? Just save the money I have left. Now here is the hard part. I still have so much more to tell her. I wonder if I should fill her in on all the details face-to-face. Maybe it's better for me to tell her what I want now. I need to know if she is willing to take a step together."

*

The next week was filled with Allen reading and studying in the library. Besides preparing for his upcoming exams, he kept few outside activities. In five days, Allen completed the seven chapters needed for his Biology and Chemistry classes. He wrote three papers, getting his other two courses out of the way. "Now all I have to do is concentrate on passing my Finnish test."

Allen found that his energy level was not as high as on his first arrival. He attributed it to the weaning daylight hours. The sun would not appear, settling behind dark clouds until around 11 am; the sky would be a hazy gray mist until about 3 pm; then, it would be night time again. He heard that people became depressed in the colder months due to lack of sunlight. The sauna was the pick up he needed to get through the cold dark hours. He started going to the largest sauna in Emmannatie, located on the roof of his building. One evening after splashing the hot rocks to over 140 degrees; he ventured to the outside part of the sauna that was on the roof. His feet were making wet tracks in the snow. He put back on his clothes realizing that the sauna was not good only for relaxation but building an internal heat for the cold Finnish air.

His Finnish test was tomorrow. There was one last chapter review. "Before I finish that, I need to send an email to Cynthia. I wonder has she written me."

He took the bus to the computer lab finding a computer immediately. He typed in his password to his email account, finding to his surprise, two messages from Cynthia. She invited him to come anytime, it was up to him. "Yes," he thought, "I will be there soon." He wrote her a quick line telling her he would call later.

"Now I got something to say about this experience." He looked over the school directory, trying to determine if he could send his email to everyone on the system. Having formed so many new friendships he began typing his goodbye letter.

The Life and Times of Allen Court

~

'It's Allen signing on and out for the last time to my study abroad people. During my stay here, I had the opportunity to meet so many foreign and exchange students. I'm glad for the opportunity to meet you, and briefly share parts of your culture and life as I shared mine. You have made an impact on me and how I define and re-define the world. The experiences here have broadened my knowledge of the world. Through personal experiences, I've had to re-evaluate my own thought process and the impact that it has on shaping the world I live in.

   Some of us are leaving, and others are coming back. I'm one of those who will be leaving, but I had spoke with some of you about future meetings and hopefully, we may have the opportunity to see each other again. So, for those who I may not see before I leave. I am emailing you a hood rich send off.

   First of all, I would like to send a shout out to all of my party people: a.k.a. Bounce Click, a.k.a. French Connection, a.k.a. Sweden voyage entourage. To Dr. Jekyll and Mr. Hyde-Steffan, leave the vodka alone!

   What up to that sly cat Daniel, my ace, I would like to say, gracias, por el espanol. One of the first cats, I walked around town with and we traveled to Stockholm together.

   Can't forget that suave player, Raheem. Gave me the low-low on what goes down in J-town. We set it off in Tampere!

   Can't forget that forever-dancing German girl. Disco fever Melanie, and her pretty little friend, Natalia-thanks for the hook up on Roma.

   Future Hugo Boss model Julien; When you get back to Paris, remember that song we use to sing,' them girls thinking that they dimes but they only some nickels…you know the rest!"

To Fernando, hooking up the Italian dishes. To Taz and Vivian, I better not catch you two dancing on tables. Now for all of you that were not mentioned. Wait for the sequel. But, seriously, I'm just trying to say I will remember you all. Till we rest where it all begins. Allen.

Allen pressed the send button; then rushed to catch the bus back to his apartment. He had called Saga to help him with his Finnish lesson earlier that day. He arrived back to his apartment late. She had arrived early. He saw her as she walked to the front door of his building, he was right behind her.

"What up, candy girl?" He said approaching quickly. She turned and smiled at him.

"Hi." she responded. "I thought you would be in your room."

"No, I had to get out and quiet my mind a bit. I just came from the lab." They took the stairs going to his apartment. She settled down on his bed seeing all the papers scattered across his covers.

"You've been studying. I see."

"Trying to. What's been happening with you since I been away?"

"Doing the same old thing, work, school, nothing too interesting. I saw a couple of good movies. One, with a guy called "The Dude," in it."

"The who?" Allen asked; Saga continued.

"Yeah, it was a great movie. I wouldn't mind seeing it again. You want to go this weekend?"

"Yeah, I can go. I haven't been in the mood for doing much. My last test is tomorrow. Speaking of, I have some studying to do."

They reviewed vocabulary and numbers.

The Life and Times of Allen Court

Allen sensed that Saga wanted more. He knew that initially, there relationship had been a physical one; but it had also developed into a real friendship. He enjoyed their conversations; she brought insight into certain aspects of Finnish life that he would not have realized without her.

Allen focused his attention on his work, as she sat near him. He knew from earlier experience, that no matter how much she wanted him, he had to be the initiator. She waited for a move that never came.

"I have had enough of studying. I'm ready for the test. I'm going to go bed early." Saga exhaled, disappointed. She stood up to leave. "I'm tired myself," she said.

"You still want to go to the movies, right?" Allen asked.

"Yeah, this Friday."

"If it's cool, we can go after my test tomorrow," he told her. She smiled, leaned forward and kissed him on the cheek; as he sat. "I take that for a yes."

"Tomorrow is good. I'll see you later Allen." She left his room. "That is the first time I've seen her step forward like that," he thought.

He got up and opened his door. He watched her as she disappeared around the hallway. Looking out for a moment, he returned to his room and shut the door. Sitting on his bed he looked out the window. His eyes followed Saga...until she disappeared in the distance.

~

Allen waited in front of the movie theater. The test had gone by smoothly. It contained three parts. In the first section, he had to listen to a man speak in Finnish and translate the phrases. The second part was direct questions, where he answered vocabulary questions

on paper. The third and last part, he was given a choice
of three pictures and had to communicate what was going
on in each picture. He passed, grateful that it was finally
over. Saga appeared before him snapping him from his
thoughts of the test into to the present.

"So how did you do?" She asked excited.

"I passed."

"I knew you would. You want to get something
to eat?" They walked over across the street into a small
pizza buffet and sat at a small booth talking of the time
that passed from summer to winter.

"I've learned a lot since from being here. I'm glad
I met you."

"Really?" Saga sounded it as if she was shocked.
"You know I am glad too." I know that when I am with
you, I think about things that I normally wouldn't or at
least think about things from a different perspective." She
told him.

"I have to say you do the same for me." He bit
into his pizza knowing that Saga's feelings for him had
only increased. "How can I let her down? It hurts me to
tell her goodbye; but I have to." His thoughts were
getting the better of him.

"I really like you and value your friendship, but
you know; I'm leaving in a few days." He saw a quick
break in her eyes as her shoulders sank. Realizing what
she had just done, she brought her body to full attention,
staying strong.

"I knew… you weren't staying here forever." She
tried to smile. "When you get back home, keep in
touch."

Allen nodded, knowing that whatever he did to
keep in touch it, it would never be enough.

"I will try; one way or another. Come on let's see
the movie."

The Life and Times of Allen Court

*

His feelings of letting Saga down interfered with him enjoying the movie. Allen was filled with too many emotions to truly explain why he felt the way he did. "School is over. I've made all these travel plans to see Cynthia in Egypt. Egypt, I am going to be in Egypt in less than a week! I reserved a flight to see Cynthia in a few days." Saga's laughter brought him back to the movie for a moment. He leaned back in the seat, exhausted from his thoughts. The movie ended, Saga wanted to come back to his apartment. Allen declined, telling her he needed some time for himself.

He was going to be traveling alone on a trip unlike any before. He had always had someone with him covering the things that he may have left behind. However, with all of his preparation, Allen was confident that he would make it through. He hugged Saga for the last time.

"I'll be in touch. But, not until I return back to the states." He kissed her on her cheek.

"Will you remember me?" She asked.

"Well, let me see…considering how cute, how smart, and how kind hearted and sexy you are; and you put up with someone like me. It may be difficult…but I just may find it very, very hard to forget you." He looked at her seriously. "You don't have to ask that question." They hugged for a moment; releasing each other, slowly.

"Goodbye, Allen." Saga began to walk away. Allen watched as the distance between them grew.

"Hey, Saga." She turned around as he shouted. "I'll miss you." She waved goodbye to him, and then turned away. Allen stared at her as she walked off.

"I can't believe, I didn't see that. All this time she was in love with me! It wasn't until now, that I realize it.

I'm just as blind as the next person sometimes. Saga was the truth. Everyday, I've been thinking about this-or-that and it was with me all this time. Saga was one of my best teachers."

"Thank you," he said aloud, as he walked back to his apartment.

~

"Don't mind the flat tire in the back that helps with the traction when going over rocks." Allen fought back his laughter; he continued speaking to the German man.

Allen had sent out an email stating that he had a bike and television up for sale. A transfer student had called interested in the bike. Three people had looked at the bike yet it would not sell. He was determined to get rid of it today.

"Look, I'm going to show you myself." Allen hopped on the bike with the wheel sagging. "Just needs a little air." The man looked perplexed. Allen took off riding in a circle. "See it works brakes and all."

He took one hand and pointed to the broken back reflector.

"That there, gives your bike, character. Sure to get lots of attention." Allen began to laugh. He got off the bike and looked at it thinking, 'Just give it away.'

"You know, I really like it, but, I can't take it with me. So…"

"I'll take it." The man said calmly.

"So I'm just going to… You'll what? You want it?" The man pulled out the money and handed it to Allen. Placing his hands on the handlebars; he pushed the bike away.

"That's one thing down." He had met a girl earlier who bought the television. He gave his speakers to Julien and spoke with Salaam about keeping his receiver. Allen carried the receiver over to Salaam's room. He was buzzed in and sat down with Salaam.

"How are you, my friend?" Salaam asked Allen as he came in the door.

"I'm doing good getting ready to leave, you know."

"Man, that's right. I wish you could stay a little longer."

"Me too, but, I got to go home. This trip was good for traveling and meeting new; but, I still have to complete my work for the end result."

"Yeah, I understand. I understand." Salaam nodded.

"Anyway, I'll give you one last fade. This one's for gratis." Salaam grabbed his clippers. Allen cut his hair in twenty minutes. "Man that's half the time it takes for Raheem. I have to meet up with him later tonight." He told Salaam.

"I have to go. Be easy. I know I'll see you again."

"Peace, young brother. I'll miss not having you around."

Allen hurried to his room. On the way he bumped into Fernando.

"Fernando." Allen caught their attention. They stopped for a moment.

"How was St. Petersburg?" Allen asked.

"Great city."

"If they are back, that means Daniel should be too. Most definitely, have to see him while I still have the chance. First things first, have to call my dog." Allen rumbled through his phone book finding Raheem's number.

"Rah' what's up!"

"What up playboy. What you up to?"

"Running around getting things together before I leave."

"Damn, you are leaving! How soon are you going?"

"In about, two days."

"I'll stop by in an hour."

"Cool. I'll see you then." Allen hung up the phone. Finding his camera he headed up stairs to see if Daniel had arrived. After knocking twice, Daniel came to the door.

"How are you?" Allen asked.

"Good and you?"

"Feeling fine." Allen walked in as Daniel went over to his backpack.

"How was your trip?" Allen asked. Daniel nodded his head slowly.

"It was really nice. The group went to St. Petersburg and Moscow. Moscow was nice but, St. Petersburg is the more beautiful of the two." Daniel told him.

"Talk to any chicas?" Allen asked joking with him.

"Yes." Daniel laughed. "I went to a club and had two blondes. One in front of me and one behind me; I grabbed one and…" Daniel made a pinching motion with his fingers. "Then she grabbed me."

"You had a good time?"

"There are a lot of nice things to see. The only thing is the people are so poor. We would leave a place and crowds of people would beg us for money." Daniel walked back to his desk. "Look, I got something to show you."

He pulled a black rubber helmet with two long straps from his bag. "This is a World War II airplane fighter helmet."

145

"Good one." Allen said. "I wanted to get a picture before I go. I'm leaving tomorrow."

"My friend, have safe travels; you have my email?"

"Yeah, I got all that. I'll be in touch in a couple of months when I return home."

"Goodbye."

Allen hugged him and turned to leave. On exiting Daniel's room, he saw Raffia standing near the stairs. "So I can't speak English, hugh?" He chuckled to himself. Allen began heading for his floor when Raffia called out to him.

"Allen. I know you are leaving soon, do you think you can come by before you leave."

"Yeah, I can come by in a couple of hours, say around ten. Is that cool?" She smiled.

"Yes, I will cook something for you."

"You don't have to do all of that. I tell you now, I won't be able to stay long I have some final packing to do."

"Just stop by." He nodded and walked down the stairs. "No changing my rules now! I'm not going to do anything with her this late in the game." He reassured himself. He opened up the door of his apartment thinking of the clothes he still had to pack. Most of his clothes were already packed. His Adidas bag still burst over with clothes from his Stockholm trip.

The doorbell rang. Raheem entered the room.

"What up. You're just in time. I don't have enough room for some of this stuff so you may be the winner of it." Allen told him.

"That's cool let me get that Polo hat." Raheem wasted no time.

"I guess I can let you have it… What's the word with Zaleha. I haven't heard from her in a while."

"I told you about Zaleha, man. She's moved on to someone else."

"I ain't asking out of want; I just wanted to know how she is. I was hoping we could at least be friends."

"I feel you on that one." Raheem said trying on one of the shirts. "Yeah, this looks good on me." Allen ignored his comments.

"And then there was my girl Saga. Man, I didn't see that one coming." Allen confessed.

"Yeah, you were sleep walking on that one. She was diggin' on you. I ran into her once and her whole conversation was Allen this, Allen that. Ha,ha, ha." Raheem laughed much to the annoyance of Allen.

"Shut up, man. You're right but I don't need that right now." Allen laughed along with him. "Guess who invited me up, today?" Allen said comically. "Raffia."

Raheem laughed as Allen nodded his head talking. "She knows a brothers leaving tomorrow, she wants to give me some go away lovin." Allen told him. "But I won't be able to do it. So Superman, I'm gonna let you don the cape and play captain save'em."

"What do you mean?" Raheem grinned. "You're not going to hit it."

"It's too late in the game for that, but..." Allen said. Raheem nodded, looking at his watch.

"I got time." Raheem

"I know you do." They started laughing. .

"Anyways." Raheem looked at him slyly. "I already have an appointment."

"What?" Allen asked surprise.

"I ran into her too. She told me to come by tomorrow." Raheem boasted.

"Do your thing. You can don the cape and play captain save 'em.' As for me, I'm going to go up and eat with her later tonight."

"Yeah, I bet! I know what you're going to eat."

"Whatever.."

"I'm going to miss you, dog. We got to stay in touch."

"I'm going to miss being here. I got real comfortable here, after I adjusted. But, nothing last forever, still, I know we are going to stay in touch and I will come back someday."

"Peace, black." Allen said as Raheem waked out the door.

He waited a moment before going upstairs to Raffia's. "So many good-byes today; too many good-byes. But it's only temporary, right?" He knew in his heart it would never be the same. "I have no regrets about coming here. There are few things in life a person can say they have no regrets about doing. The sacrifices that I have made for once have all made sense. To think that is not even over yet just turning into something else. I clearly see that I'm a creator in my life." Allen walked out the door. "What does Raffia have waiting for me?" He knocked on her door twice. When he turned to leave the door swung open.

"Hey."

"Hi Raffia, what's going on?" Allen asked not entering the room.

"I just finished cooking, do you want some pasta?"

"It's hard for me to turn down authentic, Italian cooking." He walked in the door. The small kitchen was a mess, with dirty pans hovering on the stove. The tiny sink was loaded with dishes. He walked into her room for the first time she had left it plain, with only a few pictures on her wall. Allen sat down as Raffia gathered two plates. She walked into the room carrying two small plates of plain pasta. Allen ate the spaghetti happily. He reminisced on the first night meeting each other.

"You told me I can't speak English. You are off the wall." Allen told her.

"At the time I could not understand as well as I do now." Raffia explained. "Now I can follow you well." She looked at him quietly, reminding him of a look that Scarlen had given him. "I liked what you wrote in you're email." She told him.

"Thank you." He turned and looked at the flashing clock on her desk. It blinked 11:37p.m.

"If that is the correct time, I've got to go." Allen stood up to leave. "It was good knowing you." He said as he turned to walk out. "Good-bye Raffia."

"Good bye, Allen." He turned surprised that she had said his name fully.

"This is good-bye." He hugged her.

"Chow." He walked down the stairs. "A day full of memories and a night full of goodbyes."

*

Allen woke up in the morning, feeling anxious. The room was bare now, just as it was the day he had moved in. Only his backpack and bags in the corner interrupted the monotony of the room. Leaving the door open, he walked over to the main hall to return his room key. The halls where littered with extra mattress and wooden frames. Time was moving faster than he was.

"I have to get to the station in a half an hour. A lot of students are going to the station to see us off. He had received a phone call from Scott saying that they all would take cabs to the train station at 2:00 p.m." He did a final check up, taking all money and cards. While looking out the window, two taxis pulled up. Allen hurried to the elevator, bringing his large backpack and Adidas duffel bag with him downstairs. He met Scott at the elevator; Scott helped Trisha with her things. He looked at Scott;

there was seriousness in his behavior that he never had seen anytime before.

"How are you, Allen?" He said firmly.

"I'm, I'm…" He struggled with the normal casual retort. His feelings were twisted inside. He was leaving his newfound friendships and had no idea what the next month would bring. Traveling with no safety net, all of these thoughts had gathered momentum as his final goodbyes to Finland took place. He paused for a moment as Scott looked at him with a similar anxiety on his face.

"…leaving."

Scott nodded, telling him that he understood. Scott was silent as Trisha stood joking in the elevator with the Belgium girl that had accompanied them to Stockholm.

"What was the Belgium girl's name?" Allen asked himself. "What is her name?" He repeated louder in his head. "What does it matter, in less than an hour you won't ever see her again. That is exactly why? I can at least remember her name." The girl looked at him and smiled.

"Hi, Allen." The girl said to him. 'She told me once, I know it! It will come.'

"Hi, Lauren."

"So you're leaving today also?" Lauren asked him. Allen nodded at her then looked at Trisha. She stood smiling, wiping her sandy blond hair from her eyes. He looked closer and saw that she was fighting back tears.

"This is going to be one." Allen thought as the elevator reached the main floor.

They got out the elevator and there stood a group of the foreign students. Scott started speaking with his old roommate, the Portuguese kid that Allen had met on the night of his arrival. Allen put his bag down as Ben approached him.

150

"Have a safe trip home."

"Thanks."

"Let me help you with that." Ben said, picking up the duffel bag and placing it into the back of the cab. His girlfriend came around the corner and hugged Allen goodbye.

"I have to go upstairs and get one other bag, I'll be right back." Allen motioned to Scott before sprinting to the elevator. He just missed it. He bounced up the steps running to his room walking through for the last time. He took the television from his dresser and placed it outside the room door. Allen looked at the silent room.

'It looks just as empty as the day I arrived; but if I close my eyes it all changes for me. How things can change in one day.' Hearing a honk, it brought him back to the present. He walked out the room letting the door close itself.

"Goodbye." Allen reached the bottom of the stairs. Some of the people that had been downstairs had jumped into cabs. Scott had saved a place for Allen with him and Trisha. Trisha now was completely silent, looking at every building, glancing at the streets, the signs.

Allen was doing the same thing, looking at the ice along the leaves of the trees. He focused his attention on the windshield watching the snowflakes transform into wet splashes. The taxi climbed the streets getting closer to the train station. Allen remembered walking the streets with friends. Warm memories repelled the winter cold, thinking back to the summer of his arrival. The taxi pulled into the station. The group took out their bags and walked into the station.

In the hallway, waiting, were over twenty students. As soon as they walked in, they found themselves in a circle of hugs and good-byes. Allen hugged Mari and Jean from the French Connection. He hugged two other people he had only met and spoke with

151

a couple of times before. There was a variety of familiar faces he realized he would never see again. Sadness fully rested upon him. He looked at the time and motioned to Scott that they had to go. Trisha was in the middle of three different conversations writing down numbers and address at a frantic pace.

Scott was the first to walk out onto the train. Allen followed with Trisha having her bags carried by a tall Finnish man. The train whistle blew signaling it was time to leave. Allen had laid his bags in a seat with Scott and Trisha following suit. They all went back to the passenger door and waved to the group as the train pulled off. Trisha could not hold back any longer, she began to cry. The train moved away; slowly, and then gathered momentum. The man that had helped Trisha with her bags ran along side the train waving, causing Trisha to laugh through her tears. The train picked up speed, leaving them all behind. Trisha and Scott went back to their seats. Allen sat adjacent from them. Scott wrapped his arm around Trisha's shoulder while she cried. She talked between her tears. Scott sat consoling Trisha as she held her head down. He squeezed her shoulder to comfort her.

The train cabin was silent. Allen held his head.

"I miss them already. I miss the newness of the experiences. Will I catch that feeling again?" He closed his eyes, and buried the back of his head into the headrest.

Chapter 12
Egypt

The flight from Helsinki to London took three hours. Allen had a two hour layover in London Heathrow Airport. The flight from London to Cairo was a little over six hours. He had called Cynthia upon arrival; she told him to meet her in Aswan. "Just like her," he thought cynically, "I fly five thousand miles to see her, she tells me to go five hundred more." Cynthia had already booked a hotel two nights for him in the city and had arranged for someone to pick him up at the gate.

She told him to visit Cairo, solo, and then they could travel; together later. She had been called to finish a research project in Aswan, Egypt; but promised to make up for the two day diversion with a small boat ride later. She told him the boats were called feluccas.

Allen had asked, 'what was a felucca?' She told him that the felucca was the small boats that have floated upon the Nile since the days of the pharaohs. She would be staying at a small apartment outside of the city of Karnak. After three days she would be finished and could spend most of her time with him.

"I can understand, but I'm still upset." He told her. "I wanted to see you first thing when I got here."

"Why is that?" She responded playfully hoping to elicit some kind of sentiment from him. "There are plenty of things for you to see or do."

"I didn't come all this way to be playing around." He said seriously.

"Well, what did you come for?" Again, she was coy.

"I came to see…" Allen paused for a moment thinking to himself. "What do you want me to do; wear my heart on my sleeve?" He thought, before finishing his sentence…the pyramids."

"What!" Cynthia shouted, "You're so stubborn." She told him. Allen laughed.

'Just like old times.' He thought.

"Look, name calling is not how good couples fight." Allen responded calmly.

"So you want to be a couple now?" She questioned him calming down.

'Now, you're starting to hear me." He told her. She paused for a moment.

"We can continue this when we see each other. You should go to the Museum of Egyptian Antiquities in Cairo. The third gold sarcophagus weighs over 230lbs of solid gold. And the other coffins are covered in red rubies and blue lapis. You should see all the details of the wings of Isis that cover the coffin." Cynthia went on and on. Allen listened on and smiled. "Be careful and have fun while you are traveling through Cairo. If you try to buy anything remember, most things are negotiable. Do your best," Cynthia said before hanging up the phone.

"What is that about?" he asked her.

"You are going to have to see for yourself. There's a lot of interesting things too see and whatever you go through, it's worth it. I'm just letting you know you're going to meet a lot of nice people but don't get too upset with anyone. Call me when you get to the hotel. I'll see you soon, Allen."

'Now I have to travel through this without her,' he thought. "I'll try to make the most of it." He told her.

He gathered up his bags at the baggage claim and followed the signs out. The people around him marched along in silence. He walked past a staircase, feeling woozy from the tension in his stomach. An Arab man leaning on a stairway rail greeted him.

"Al-Salaam Alaikum." The man said.

"Wa Alaikum assalam." Allen responded.

Allen kept walking, before long he was swarmed with people trying to get him to come to their respective hotels. A short, Arab man, in an old navy-blue suit walked up to Allen. He was holding a sign with his last name on it.

"My friend, my friend. How are you today?" Not wanting to be rude Allen nodded. He turned his head taking in his surroundings. He noticed more people like the man next to him, walking alongside passengers as they left the passport control station.

"My friend, my friend." The small man tried to redirect Allen's attention to himself. "There is a five dollar fee for the cab ride." Mr. Blue suit told him. Three young boys came by grabbing the passengers' bags. Allen picked up his Adidas bag before one boy grabbed the handle.

"I will, I will." Allen tried telling the boy that he could carry it himself, but the boy insisted. They walked outside of the airport walking about 100 feet to rows of older cars and black vans. The boy neared the back of a van where another teenager opened up the back doors.

"*Baksheesh! Baksheesh!*" The boy turned and said to Allen, holding his hand outstretched, in case he didn't understand. 'He wants a tip,' Allen thought.

He reached in his pocket and handed him a dollar, he seemed unsatisfied. The other visitors were going through the same thing. Allen ignored it all and took the front seat of the van.

"What was the Arabic word for no thanks? *La shukran.*" He remembered, "I may have to say that a lot here."

155

The Life and Times of Allen Court

"They'll take you to the hotel, it's the last stop."
Mr. Blue Suit told him. The other passengers piled in the van, speaking in French. The driver started the engine of the van, Allen's emotions changed from nervousness to excitement. The van lurched forward and spun out of the parking lot. Allen looked out of the front window. The road ahead opened toward the desert. He could see a highway, forming miles ahead of him. Allen rolled the window down enjoying the sight of a swaying balm tree as the wind shifted through it.

The van floated upon the highway, high over the sands. He looked over at a faded soda advertisement; a pretty Arabic woman smiled next to a glass bottle. The van moved deeper in the city of Cairo. Allen looked upon apartment buildings that were decades old. The van exited the highway rolling near a police station. Allen noticed a large palm tree near a fountain in the center of the road. It was close to two a.m. and the streets were still busy with honking cars. The van made a turn and the driver motion to the French passengers in the back. Allen had directed so much of his attention to the sights that he forgot about the people behind him.

The passengers left the van, the driver helped them with their bags. Allen had tried to ask the driver a few questions but only got a shy grin.

"My English, not so good." The man shook his head as he replied. Allen turned his attention to the action taking place along the street. People were in long, loose-flowing clothes. Groups of people where gathered on the street, calmly eating dates. Others jumped around waving their hands around in the air as if to get the person's attention. The driver made a sudden turn, passing a nightstand vendor who sold noodles and gyros. Allen looked up and saw that the sign read, 'Ciao Hotel.' Mr. Blue Suit had shown him a picture of the hotel.

156

Meshawn Deberry

The driver had gathered his bags and walked in the hotel with them. The receptionist was a young girl. She reminded him of someone, but he could not think of whom at the moment. The driver and the girl conversed in Arabic for a moment until a bell hop came to pick up Allen things. The girl spoke to Allen saying had been paid for.

The driver was still waiting by the side of the desk, watching as they exchanged their dialogue. The bellhop came by taking his bags. Allen walked over to an elevator that was behind the reception counter. The metallic door opened. The young bellhop walked in first holding his bags. They went up two flights and stopped with a large shake. The bell hop walked out first. As he walked behind him, Allen heard a man talking in an Australian accent. An Indian man, looking just a bit older than Allen walked behind the Australian listening intensely. The Australian spoke of the trips he had already taken around Egypt. He mentioned Aswan and Luxor and sparking Allen's conversation.

"Pardon me, I just got here, but I want to talk to you about traveling around in this country."

"You would do better designing your own trip. You'll come out spending less money. It's easy once you know where to go and what to expect." He told him.

"I'm about to go out for about an hour but come by either tonight or tomorrow morning. I'm leaving for Israel tomorrow afternoon."

"What's your name?"

"Jim."

"Allen. And you?" He asked the Indian man.

"Amir."

"I may see you both later as well."

Allen walked to his room the door. The bellhop gave Allen his room key.

"Thanks." He turned the key and walked in. He could see the bed directly in front of him. Allen walked around the room. The bathroom was adjacent to the bed. He walked in and was pleased. Allen surveyed the room one more time and began to unpack some of his clothes.

"What should I"… the phone rang stopping his thoughts.

"Now, who is this?" Allen said out loud, he located the sound. Recognizing an old rotary phone, while inspecting the phone, it rang again. "Should I answer this?" The phone continued ringing. Allen lifted the receiver to his ear.

"Who is this?"

"You have a meeting with a tour guide upstairs!" A woman exclaimed.

"Who is this?" he repeated.

"This is the front desk! You have a meeting with a tour counselor upstairs on the fifth floor. His name is John." Allen was confused at her insistence.

"I didn't set up any meetings?"

"All right. I might as well see this person. He can give me a reference point on the prices here." Allen thought.

"He's waiting now! Are you leaving?" She demanded.

"Yeah! Give me a minute, I'll be there shortly."

"John is waiting!" She insisted.

"All right!" He said, putting down the phone.

~

John sat across from Allen, lifting his cigarette slowly to his mouth. His eyes directly focused on Allen John scrutinized his American guest. The restaurant was located at the top floor of the hotel. John had waved Allen to his table as soon as he walked through the door.

After Allen sat at the table, he offered him some food while he explained his travel packages. Allen agreed to hear him out. His first offer sounded perfect. His first two days would be in Cairo where he would have his own personal cab driver to take him to Saqqara Pyramids, the Egyptian Papyrus museum and then to the Pyramids of Giza. The next day he was to go to the Egyptian tower and then the Egyptian Museum. Later that night, on the second day, he would have a first class train ticket to Aswan with a three day first class reservation cruise along the Nile with two nights in a first class hotel and then back to Cairo.

Allen had to remind himself, "I only need two days here. The prices he gave me are cool but the only thing I would like is the personal cab." Allen negotiated with him for fifteen minutes between bites of his sandwich and cola.

"Look that is too much money for me to pay." He continued talking with the man going lower as the time stretched on. He finally got the coordinator down to a decent price. "I know that I'm still getting hustled, but right now I'll go along with it." He planned out his goals for the next day. "I need to get out and see how much I can work this thing out myself. I won't have to worry about the trains with the cab driver."

He finished the food with the man still looking at him with questioning eyes. John took a careful pull from the cigarette, blowing the smoke out the side of his mouth.

Allen finished his food, standing up to leave the table.

"How much is that?" Allen asked, John waved it off. The waiter walked by and Allen gave him the money he intended for the food.

"The receptionist will call you in the morning. Please be ready." John said leaving the table. "Tomorrow, at seven."

Chapter 13
The Pyramids

Allen awoke in the morning to the phone ringing. "Who is this? It better not be that same chick from last night." He thought picking up the phone receiver, never leaving his bed.

"Hello."

"Do you know what time it is?" The receptionist said.

"Oh no, it's her!" Allen thought. "No, I don't. But, I bet you're not going to hesitate to tell me."

"It's now eight-thirty! Your driver has been waiting for over an hour. Are you coming now?" Her voice had not toned down, since the night before. Allen rolled over with the phone to his ear.

"Yeah, I will be down in a few minutes I have to get some breakfast first."

"Make it quick. There's some one waiting for you!"

"Goodbye." Allen put on his jeans and a took out a baseball jersey from his bag. He went upstairs to the dining area. The hall had tables upon tables of tourists. Allen waited in line. He picked an orange, and a small slice of golden honey cake with tea. As he walked, two cute Asian girls waved him over. "Let me see what they're about." Allen walked over and sat at their table.

"My name is Charlene."

"And I'm Tasanee." Allen shook both of their hands.

"I'm Allen."

"You're from the United States aren't you?" Charlene said, leaving no spaces between her breaths. Allen shook his head yes. Charlene clapped.

"See I told you." she said to her friend. "Tasanee thought you were from Jamaica." Tasanee nodded.

"And, where are you from?" Allen asked.

"We're from Thailand." Tasanee said energetically. "We come here for fun. We've been here for four days. We've been having a good time. Today will be our first day out by our selves."

"Really? I have some cab driver to take me around Cairo today."

"Oh, who is your driver?" Charlene asked.

"I don't know yet." Allen thought about it. "You mean to say, they have a number of them?"

"Yes. We've had two so far. But, now we…" Tasasnee began as is she wanted to say something more, paused for a moment. "…we just decided to see what things would be like on our own." Charlene agreed. Allen had finished his food.

"If you don't mind; I'm leaving now. Are you going downstairs?"

"We're leaving." They took the elevator to the lobby. They walked out, Allen saw an Arabic man in his late forties, leaning against the lobby desk. He was wearing a black leather coat and smoking a cigarette. Charlene and Tasanee waved to him soon as they saw his face.

"Sy." The women sounded like a choir.

"Hey, girls." The man said to the women.

The Life and Times of Allen Court

Allen turned to be greeted by the leering counter girl.

"You see, Sal has been here for over an hour waiting for you! And you, you're just taking your time." Allen turned to the man who had spoken with the girl.

"My name is Allen. I guess I have kept you waiting long enough." Sal nodded. "Hey, you need a ride into town?"

Allen asked Charlene and Tasanee. The girls said yes.

"Sal, can we drop them off?" Allen asked him.

"Yes, it's not a problem." They walked outside and got into a rusty, black Mercedes from the fifties. The black leather seats were rigid. The engine coughed, as it began to heat up. The car screeched as Sal shifted into reverse, pulling away from the hotel. The tailpipe hiccupped black smoke, as they rode along the street.

The girls chatted happily as Allen took his first daytime look at the chaotic city. People were crowded along the sidewalks. Stopping customers bartered with vendors, hands constantly moved between transactions; physical reactions matching their verbal exchanges. As they drove by corners, Allen saw beggars by trash barrels, receiving no sympathy. He focused his attention on the traffic. The cars came in two colors, rusty black or a dust covered white.

The traffic was heavier, heading into the city. The cars drove only inches from each other, cutting the other off at every opportunity. Sal made hand gestures at various people. Sal would angrily curse in Arabic to any 'offending,' passing driver then speak casually in English to Allen. Allen saw a group of people eating pita sandwiches.

"Are those any good?" Allen asked him. Sal laughed.

"No. It's donkey. I don't think its beef, it's too cheap. So, you are from America." Sal said grinning out the window his words spilling over. "It's a good place! People live well there!" A mid seventies black Volvo, swerved ahead of them, causing Sal to veer off. Sal began yelling out Arabic obscenities. He continued for twenty seconds.

"You want me to drive?" Allen asked him. "That is the fourth car that we nearly ran into."

"Oh sorry, sorry." Sal said, turning around a tall balm tree that stood in the middle of the road. "I was here yesterday." Allen thought. "This must be a major part of town." Sal pulled the car along the side, letting Charlene and Tasanee out.

"Bye, Allen. Hey! If you want, come by our room, its 252. "

"Yeah, will do." He said closing the doors.

"Bye, Sy." They waved to the cab driver as he pulled off.

"Nice girls, aren't they? Allen said.

"Yes, they're very nice." Sal said, as he pulled away. Sal turned off the main road towards the expressway.

Allen fiddled through his bag picking up his CD player. The car floated as it hit a highway overpass. Allen saw the open Sahara Desert before him. He was about to put in the CD but stood still in amazement as the Great Pyramids of Giza lay before him. For a moment he had lost his breath. He looked upon in silence as they car drove past. He instantly remembered the first time seeing them (in pictures as a child) now looking at them in person. Allen told Sal to stop.

"Why are we going past them? We need to go there."

"Yes, we're going to go, but later." Sal nodded. "Now we're going to the Saqqara pyramids."

"Saqqara?" Allen questioned him. "I want to go to Giza. Take me to the Sphinx!" The car had begun to pass the pyramids. "Man! What's going on?"

"Don't worry! Don't worry! We go to the Saqqara pyramids these are the first pyramids. We will go to the Giza pyramids, don't worry." Sal tried to console Allen.

"I had better get there!"

*

"Now, when you go down the stairs, do not give anybody money. Remember do not give anyone, anything. Not one baksheesh! Just buy your ticket and give it to the man at the door." Sal told Allen as he walked him along to the pyramids. He could see the large step pyramid to the left of him. Similar to the Mayan pyramids. These were the oldest pyramids of Egypt. They stopped at the ticket booth.

"I'll be here when you have finished," said Sal. Allen bought a ticket and headed to an underground tomb. He walked down the steps; there was a lone Arabic man in a dark tunic walking in front of him. He could hear an English speaking tour guide in a chamber below. Allen reached the room where a large, black sarcophagus stood in the center of the room. Etched hieroglyphics aligned the wall. A French tour guide was leading a small group of four around the room, explaining the meanings of the writing. He pointed to the sarcophagus, saying that it had been taken from granite rock that could only be found in Aswan. The rock was then molded into the large sarcophagus for the deceased pharaoh. The guide left with the group; leaving only him and the Arab man in the room. The man walked over to Allen pointing at the same thing the tour guide had. Allen was about to leave the man pointed to a corner. Allen took a closer look and could see that it led to a

164

small chamber. He thanked the man for the help. The man stood with his hand out.

"Oh, you want some money?" Allen dug into his pocket pulling out an Egyptian note reading the number five. He handed it to him. "How much money have I given him?' Sal told me not to give him anything but he looks so broke!" The man stayed with his hand held out with the five on top. "All right, I will give him something else." Allen gave him an American dollar bill. The man didn't blink. He continued standing with his hands out. Allen started to feel his sympathy disappear. He gave him another dollar. The man dipped his hands; gesturing for more.

"You better take that, before I decide to take it all back!" Allen said this loud enough for him to hear, not knowing if he would understand. Allen headed back outside. The man followed him nearly to the top, stopping before the entrance. Allen reached Sal.

"How was it?" Sal asked Allen.

"It was cool." Allen told him as they walked along the blistering sand. The sun shone brightly mixing with dust forming a brown haze. Allen saw that the largest step pyramid was fenced off.

"Sal, let's go to that pyramid."

"We cannot go over there; they have it closed for repairs."

"If they had closed the pyramid, why did you bring me here?" Allen asked with Sal responding with hunched shoulders.

Allen turned his attention to the desert. Along the different banks, he could see pits in the ground with patches of grass surrounding them. On the drive over Allen had seen small patches of land where people previously farmed. The fertile ground was near a muddy swamp. A crude irrigation system brought water to the land. They walked back to the car. Allen asked him again to take him to the pyramids at Giza.

"You will go! You will go! But later!" Sal reassured him. "First, you must go to the Egyptian Papyrus museum."

" Is there really such a thing?" Allen wondered, why he could not dictate the conditions of his own trip. Sal hit the road driving past the farms. Allen didn't want to be upset on a day like this.

"I just want to enjoy my time. Look at all of this. I need to share this with somebody." He leaned back in the seat as Sal looked around. They drove past a shop with a man yelling at the car. Sal slammed on the breaks, coming to a stop in the middle of the road.

"What's going on?" Allen thought as the car began to head back to the shop.

Sal began talked with the man in Arabic. Allen remained in the car.

"What is this guy doing?" Allen thought to himself. Sal continued having a conversation with the man, all the while, the man pointed at Allen. Sal walked over to the passenger window.

"Children from the villages learn how to make carpets here."

"What? I'm not interested. I want to go to the pyramids and you talking about I have to go to this museum I've never even heard of. We need to go." Allen protested.

"Please, come and have a look. Just a look, you don't have to buy anything. I want to talk with my friend for a moment." Allen left the car walking into the shop. Another man had walked out of the place. He guided Allen into a large open room. Rows of eight foot spindles lined the room. He looked at the carpet that was on the floor of the room. A large, twenty-by-fifteen multicolored carpet covered the gray floor. Finished carpets were rolled along the sides with smaller ones hung around the room.

The spindles were occupied by young girls, many no older than twelve years old weaved brilliant colors together, forming thick carpets.

"This is our school, where girls can come and learn how to make carpets."

"Looks more like a sweat shop!" Allen said leaving the man by his side walking over to one young girl. Her thin fingers looped thread at a heart racing pace.

"If you want a carpet you can purchase one here. We have very good quality."

"No thanks. I don't need one."

"No, no! Come upstairs, there's more." Allen walked up the stairs this time to see a room filled wall to wall with piles of carpets. Rich, large carpets hung along the walls. The man pointed to one.

"I can let you have that one for five thousand dollars." Allen looked in the far corner of the room; a group of Arabs locked their eyes upon him.

"Didn't you hear me downstairs?" Allen paused to make his point. "I don't want one!" The skinny man walked over to a smaller carpet.

"Take a look at this. I can let you have this for eight hundred dollars."

Allen shook his head. "They're all nice, but I don't need one."

"Okay, Okay how much are you willing to spend?" Allen scratched his head slowly, baiting him.

"Hmmm, I can spend about…nothing." The man began to get angry.

"I see, you have all the money in the world; but you want to be as cheap as possible with me." Allen ignored the man sweeping his eye along the carpets. The man continued ranting but Allen's attention had turned to a small, brown carpet with black mask designs.

167

"Anything you give goes to the village girl's education."

"Don't try to use the kids, this money goes to you!" Allen said before pointing to a carpet.

"I'll give you twenty dollars for that one." The man shut up for a moment, taking a look at where Allen had pointed; then began ranting again.

"That is a Nubian design. I can sell that for seventy five dollars!"

"Twenty."

"I can't let you have it for that! That would be a steal. No! Seventy-five!"

"Twenty!" Allen was standing firm. "I don't need it. If he says yes, I'll pick it up. There aren't many times I'll be able to get a real Nubian carpet? But at the same time, I don't need to be weighed down by more things, especially a carpet." He thought. They negotiated for another ten minutes, finally agreeing upon twenty-five dollars. He left the shop with conflicting emotions.

"I don't want this now, but by the time I get home, it would be smart to have a souvenir." They had wrapped the package up fitting it into a tight bundle. Sal was leaning against a tree, sipping from a bottle of water, alone.

"Hey Sal, look what I got!" Allen lifted up the carpet, sarcastically to him. "Let's ride!" Sal headed for the car.

~

"So this...is the papyrus museum?" Allen said walking in a basement shop. Along the wall where various size Egyptian papyrus posters. "This is nothing but a specialty shop." The pictures were all in glass frames marked in the corner with the prices handwritten in pounds. A short man with glasses came up to Allen while four men waited by the door. Allen was the solo customer in the shop. He took his time, walking around looking at the various frames. Many caught his eye; but after doing the dollar conversions, any standout posters were well over a hundred dollars. The short man began speaking with him.

"All the poster's here are real papyrus. You may see the same design on the street for cheaper, but it's only banana paper. The color doesn't last as long, nor is it as strong."

The man was doing his best to make him trust his product, but Allen already knew the hustle. He turned and looked at Sal and shook his head returning to the man.

"Do you have a student travel card?" the man asked, Allen nodded yes.

"You can take half off with your student discount."

"And the game is on!" Allen thought, looking at a picture of the elongated face of Pharaoh Akhenaton.

"He changed his name to Aton." Allen said out loud moving towards the 'Weighing of the Heart' poster. "I like that one too." He glanced at another poster called the Lovers Card. He saw another poster with a warrior shooting an arrow. "Who is that?" Allen pointed to the poster.

"That's Ramses the II."

"I'll take that one then."

"How much is all of that? In dollars"

"Four hundred." The curator said.

"Nope! I'm not spending that much for this." Allen bartered with the man bringing him down to eighty dollars. Even with the price being lowered, he felt no sense of victory. He took a piece of paper and drew a picture along the top.

"This is what I am to all of you." Allen picked up his creation holding up a stick man with a dollar sign for a head. The curator of the shop laughed out loud. Allen turned to look at the cab driver, Sal, but he held his eyes to the ground. Allen now had confirmation that he was being used, by Sal. The salesman was trying to make small talk with Allen. He paid him no attention.

"Would you like to have your family name in hieroglyphics along the side?" The salesman asks.

"You guys don't stop do you? Does it cost?"

"Yes. An extra thirty Egyptian pounds."

"Yeah, go ahead and write my name along the side of that other one."

The man scripted the names after Allen told him. They rolled up the posters for him.

"Hey Sy! Can we go now?" Sal nodded. Allen pointed for the door walking out.

Chapter 14
The tombs

"Why do you look so unhappy?" Sal asked.
"Why? You know why." Allen thought.

"I come here thinking that it like a home coming, but all I get, is people looking at me like some money tree."

"No, it's not that bad."

"From every exchange, from every place I've been today. First the tombs in Saqqara, to what just happened, now."

"You mean to say, someone tried to get money from you at the Saqqara? You should have told me, I would have gotten it back for you."

"You're my protection? You think I am intimidated by persistence. I gave because I wanted to. The only thing is the people I gave to were coming at me like I owed them." Allen said angrily.

Sal continued to drive, going across the highway again. He looked to see the pyramids before him; instantly his thoughts on the money spent left him.

"I made it at least." He thought as the sight came closer. Sal had begun to talk.

"They will be closing them soon. I believe you have an hour."

"If you had taken me in the first place I wouldn't have to rush." Allen thought, "Forget it, I am here now." Sy began talking again.

"I will take you to get a camel."

"A camel? No, I'll rather walk."

"It will cost thirty Egyptian pounds; if they try to charge you more, come to me."

The Life and Times of Allen Court

"Oh. So now you want to look out for me?" Allen said. "You must not get a commission from the camel man." Sal ignored Allen's comments.

"I will wait for you, at this same spot." Sal told him as he turned onto a small crowded street. The dingy apartments where packed with people. This is more village than city. Sheets hung up in building windows as drapes and people walked along the roads barefoot. Allen got out of the car and waited along with another tourist.

Before long, he could see two long-legged camels being led by two small Arabic boys. The boys sat the camels down by banging the back of their legs with wooden canes. One of the young boys got on the camel's back and waved for Allen to get on. Allen sat on the hump, it was covered by a thick red carpet type clothe. Allen gripped the back of the saddle mount, as the camel raised itself, by lifting its rear legs first. The sudden shift caused Allen to lean forward, pushing against the boy. The camel rose up so quickly, it felt like a jump. The forward legs came up allowing him to balance himself. The animal lurched forward, with a jolt. "I'm nearly eleven feet up in the air." Allen thought.

The boy directed the camel toward the desert. Allen could now see the pyramids peering above the town's buildings. Allen came along the edge to the town, the golden sand of the desert stretched out for miles in front of him. He could now see a small caravan of people, following a trail. Some people walked, others were riding along camels. As they walked ahead of him, he noticed the litter on the ground. Glass and plastic bottles were scattered across the desert path. The path chosen appeared to take him away from the site.

"We need to go that way!" Allen pointed in the direction of the Sphinx.

"Don't worry my friend." The boy said, trying to reassure him. "We will go there." The boy was young, but had a full mustache. The boy continued looking over his shoulder as they marched through the dessert. He noticed Allen's electric razor.

"My friend, what is that you have there?" He turned, motioning towards the bag.

"What? These?" He pointed to the clippers. The boy nodded, showing a smile.

"These are liners for my beard." Allen motioned to his face, showing the boy what he meant.

"Oh yes, I understand." The boy paused for a moment as Allen saw another camel ahead of him, walking through the desert.

"My friend." The boy said disrupting him from his thoughts. "Will you give me your clippers?" The boy asked him.

"Focus on driving us to those big rocks." Allen slapped the side of the camel, amused at his own joke. The camel neighed.

"My friend, do you think that you can give me something? Just a small gift for taking you here?" The boy repeated.

"Yeah, man I can hook you up with a little something when we get back" Allen said.

"Okay, what about your CD player?" the boy asked again. In the mists of Allen trying to hold on to his property he was only half a mile from the pyramids.

"Look!" Allen pointed to the site in excitement. He could see the three major pyramids as well as the smaller pyramids along the side of Khaf-Ra. He took out his camera and focused on a panoramic view of the tombs. On top of the camel, his range was limited. The boy swung his leg over one side and jumped off.

"Give me the camera, I'll take it for you." Allen leaned over and handed him the camera. The boy stood ten feet away, focusing the lens. Allen began barking directions.

"Okay, now make sure you get me and the pyramids and…" He waved his hands in each direction. The boy grinned as he focused the camera lens. "…now with the camera. You've got to be careful. It can be tricky if you don't focus everything right."

""Don't worry, my friend." The boy said calmly. "I'm very good with cameras because of the Japanese."

"The Japanese? If you say so." The boy rattled off four more shots. "The kid wasn't playing," he thought. "He knows how to use my camera better than I do." Allen played around with the camel, moving it along with each shot. Allen looked at the wide desert in front of him. The boy began walking back towards him.

"It will be dark soon. We need to get going." Allen looked to see the sun setting in the west. "Yeah, but we aren't going back to the village. We're going there." Allen pointed in the direction of the Khufu pyramid.

"My friend, we cannot!"

"Come on, let's go." The boy lowered the camel, and got back on top. Allen pointed for him to go directly to the pyramids.

"We don't have much time." The Pyramids began to tower in front of him, becoming larger with each step. Allen envisioned them, in their glory, thousands of years before. Originally covered in limestone, they would shine for miles on end. With the rising sun reflecting of the limestone they appeared as three enormous diamonds, with three golden capstones growing from the earth.

"My friend. We cannot go any closer." The boy warned him nervously. Allen told him to press on. The camel approached the rocks of the tomb of Men-Kau-Ra. The configuration up close was one where he could see the edges of the blocks. If he wanted, he could climb to the top. The camel shifted his foot along uneasily as it settled along the ruined rocks at the base of the pyramid.

"We cannot get any closer." the boy tried to convince him

"Closer!" Was the only response he received.

"Closer!" The boy neared the camel until the edge of the pyramid. The camels' foot was only two feet away.

"Listen. We must go before the guards come."

"I have to touch this, if only for a moment." He slid off the camel reaching over. Grabbing a hold of the rock feeling it crumble in his hand he slid off the camel quickly adjusting his body across in mid air sitting along the edge.

"We must hurry!" the boy warned him.

"Pardon me. Okay, let's go to the Sphinx." Allen told him satisfied. "For him, it's something he see's everyday. Me, I don't know when I will get to see it again." He took one step and made a small leap from the pyramid on the back of the camel. After resettling himself, they began marching to the Sphinx. Allen looked around for guards, but the sight was clear. The boy directed the camel to the Sphinx.

"Hold on!" the boy told him. Allen gripped the back of the pointed stirrup. The camel took off, galloping as fast as a horse through the sand. They approached a cavern type area. The boy maneuvered through the evacuated site.

"This is the place where people live in the graveyard." Stone tables lay broken in every direction. "Why did this kid go through here? I don't dig this at all." The kid brought through the living cemetery onto a smooth bank. To his right, he saw the weathered Sphinx head. The outline of the missing nose still did not diminish the strength of the sight.

"It's time to go." Allen gave the boy specific instructions not to go through the cemetery. They went around, taking a longer time returning to the village. Along the way back to the village, the boy asked again for his clippers, Allen still said no. He asked for the CD player, getting the same response. Allen gave him some money, to show his appreciation. Sal waited, Allen thanked the boy for his help.

"So how did you like it?" Sal asked, starting the engine.

"I really enjoyed it. The highlight of my day." Allen said quietly.

"I know you must be hungry. We can go and get something to eat, on me." Allen was surprised at his suggestion. He wondered if it was a sincere attempt of kindness or another trick he had up his sleeve.

"Let's go," Allen said to him as the car sped along the crowded streets.

*

"My friend, welcome," A fat balding Arab man said to Allen as he sat in a scented oil shop.

Sal had made good on his promise, buying Allen a small bowl of noodles. "Duped again." Allen thought calmly as he sifted through the now empty bowl. Allen waited for the man to return with the price list for the oils. Allen could smell the sweet aromas of jasmine and myrrh. All around, were large bottles of oils in beautiful glass bottles.

"What a nice place," Allen thought. The man returned, holding a tray with eight bottles of various fragrances. He sampled each of the oils. Allen was impressed by the variety of scents. Some were familiar, but richer fragrances of popular colognes he knew. The fat man went into his business speech.

"All of my oils are pure, they have no alcohol whatsoever." The man took a match and put it into the top of the bottle.

"See, if they're had been any alcohol it would have caught on fire." The man looked at Allen smiling, believing he now had a buying customer. Sal sat in the corner, not meeting Allen's gaze.

"How much are these?" Allen asked to the man's delight.

"I will show you the bottles now." The fat man rustled up and left the room.

"How are you Sal?" Allen asked him with a smile. Sal put on a false smile, wringing his hands.

"I am fine. Yes, yes." Allen took his camera from his bag. The bald man returned to the room with four various sizes of glasses, ranging from one liter to four ounces; he placed them on the table next to the oils.

"Before we go any further, could you do me a favor and take a picture of me and my cab driver." Allen asked the man holding his camera out to him.

"I'm going to buy something from you. Every other place he has taken me I bought something, and I'm a man who believes in carrying on tradition." Allen told the man.

"What's up, Sly." Allen sat next to Sal. "Mind taking a picture with your gullible, American friend?" Allen asked smiling.

"I don't know what you mean?" he said.

"Don't worry about that, let's take a picture. I buy something; we go back to the hotel, game over, deal?"

"If you want to take a picture," Sal asked "I guess its okay." Allen put his arm around his shoulder. Sal lifted his head and gave a goofball grin. The man took the picture with a confused look on his face. The flash went off suddenly. "I need to have some little fun with these cats," Allen thought.

"Okay, so how much is that big bottle right there?" Allen pointed to the glasses the man had just brought out. The man whipped out small piece of paper, reading off the price.

"That's one hundred and twenty dollars."

"That's a lot of money for some oils. What about that one?" Allen pointed to one that was half the size.

"I sell that one at seventy-five dollars."

"Dollars?" Allen questioned him. "Did you say dollars I thought we are in Egypt? Shouldn't we be talking, Egyptian pounds, not dollars?"

"Give me this one." Allen held out a vial that was nearly the size of his finger.

"How much is this?"

"That is twelve dollars." The bald man said with a confused look on his face. Allen scratched his chin.

"Tell you what? I'll take two bottles for eight dollars."

"What!" The smile on the man's face was completely gone. His mouth now twisted in anger. "I cannot sell two at that price! This is ridiculous, my oils are good!"

"Save it," Allen thought motioning to Sal. "Ready to leave?" Sal slowly stood up. The fat man quickly changed his expression.

"Wait, Wait. On second thought, I may be able to let you have one for ten dollars."

"Two for eight." Allen held up two fingers repeating the price.

"I cannot let you get two for that amount." The man insisted becoming angry again. "It's all apart of the act." Allen thought, replaying the day's episodes in his head. Earlier that day, all the salesman played the same boring role. First, they would be very friendly; then they would act as if you did them an injustice and try to intimidate you through their anger. This last visit, the game was over.

"Two for ten. That's my last offer. I don't need it. More than likely the bottles will break along the way, but just to keep today's average of being freehearted with my money consistent, I'll buy it. Maybe one of the two bottles will make it back home with me."

The man looked as if he was going to challenge him but nodded his head in agreement to the price. Allen paid the man, thanked him and walked out the store. Sal walked along silently. Cars sped by. In the street filled with gaping potholes. Sal unlocked the passenger side door, letting Allen in. Sal slid into the car, glancing at his watch.

"You want to see the laser light show at Giza?" He asked a weary Allen.

"I have to get some more money."

"You have seen enough?" Sal questioned him. Allen nodded yes. They reached the car.

"I need to go to a bank machine to pay for this tour. Do you know where one is?"

"Yes I can take you." Sal told him. They came to a stop sign passing slowly a young Arabic girl with dark black hair. She looked at Allen and waved.

"What was that about?" Allen asked Sal.

"That is a bad woman." Sal told him with a stern look out the window. Allen looked back as they left the street.

"You think it would be safe for me to go to a club tonight?"

"Hmmm, I don't think so. It can be very dangerous right now for you." The car came to a stop. Policeman where running along the sides of the street. Cars were jammed tight. Police where along both sides of the street.

"With all these circumstances, I'll take your advice on that." Allen said as Sal turned headed for the freeway.

"We'll go this way." Sal told him. They drifted along the empty highway. Sal turned off nearing the front of a bank. Sal got out the car with Allen. Allen waited as a man finished his transaction. Allen stepped up to the machine.

"It's all in Arabic!" Allen said expecting to see regular numbers. "I don't trust Sal to run me through it. I have to work from memory." He inserted his card then punched in his number. The machine pushed the card back. "Let me try again." The machine pushed the card back again.

"Sal, can you help me?" Sal came over and they walked through the steps again with the card still hanging out of the slot.

"I think you should just put it in." Sal said. Allen was hesitant.

"That will be the third time and I don't want to lose my card here!" Sal pushed the dangling card into the machine.

"Hey, what are you doing? Don't do that!" Allen was too late. The machine took the forced card.

"I can't believe you just did that! I could've done that!" Allen began walked back to the car. "Man, that's going to change everything, if I lose access to my card, how am I gonna buy my return ticket home? All I got is four hundred cash on me, and that's not enough to make my flight. I'll be stuck in Egypt!" Sal walked over to Allen as he waited by the passenger door.

"I'm sorry. Don't worry, we'll come back tomorrow and get your card."

"Take me back." Allen said calmer. He sat in the car, Sal walked slowly to his side. "I got to think about this. Who knows if they will help me get my card back? Wait, I haven't paid him yet for his day, plus I made a deal with John for some tickets. It's partly his fault the card got stuck in the machine. I'm not giving up my reserve cash. They're going to have to help me get my card back if they want their money." Allen sat silently not moving an inch. Sal looked at him as he pondered his predicament. Sal tried to calm him.

"Don't worry; tomorrow we will get your card. I know you are not a bad man. You listen to music." Allen looked at him strangely.

"Listen to music? What is this guy talking about?" he thought.

"Tomorrow, you'll see. We'll get your card." As soon as he stopped talking, a horrible clicking sound came from his throat.

"What is that?" Allen asked him. I had heard it earlier but ignored it.

"I have a problem here." Sal rubbed the bottom of his neck. "I have a daughter, at home, I take care of. She is very sick and needs medicine." I wonder, why is he telling me this now? The car pulled in front of the Ciao Hotel. Allen got out with Sal following behind him. John waited at the front desk with the bossy receptionist girl. Allen looked at her, and then changed his frown into a smile.

"You look exactly like my cousin. Your skin is just lighter." The girl gave him a strange look, but stopped her comment. John and Sal spoke to each other in Arabic with Sal explaining what happened as Allen looked at him unfazed.

'I got to play the cards I've been dealt.' Allen thought before speaking.

"Sal told you he pushed my card into the bank machine." Allen looked at Sal thinking, sorry buddy, but it's your turn to be the fool. "Now my card is stuck in the bank and I can't pay you for the trip until I get my card back. Not even for today." John turned to Sal looking irate, as he angrily spoke to Sal. He then turned to Allen.

"Tomorrow, we'll go and get you're card for you. The same time as today; Sal will take you." At that time, Charlene and Tasanee appeared.

"Hey, Allen." They sung out happily in unison, waving their hands as they walked toward the elevator.

"I'm going up to." Allen turned and shook Johns' hand, and then he looked at Sal.

"See you tomorrow."

The girls held the elevator for him.

"Just getting back?" Allen asked them. They shook their heads yes. Allen told them about what happened at the bank.

"That's too bad." Charlene said as Tasanee nodded in agreement. The elevator stopped at their floor.

"Allen, we should meet up for breakfast tomorrow. Okay?"

"Not a problem." Allen walked towards his door. "I know that it will be a lot cheaper than today was.

~

Allen woke again, to the phone ringing. "Not again," he grit his teeth in anger. The sun beamed through the window. "I must have overslept, again," He picked up the phone.

"Hey, what's up?"

"Do you know who this is? This is the front desk!" The girl spat out bitterly. "You need to come down now! Sal has been here again waiting for you. But you, you must not care about..." Allen hung up the phone.

"Shut up. It's too damn early for that." Allen stepped away from the bed the heat wrapped around his chest. The phone began to ring. "Let me see. Hmmm? Should I, or shouldn't I? Why not?"

"Good morning, love."

"Do not hang up the phone! Come down right…" Click!

"Forget that. I'm going to get something to eat with the Thai girls. Allen hurried and took a shower. Putting on his clothes, he stepped out of his room, just in time to see Charlene and Tasanee walking into the elevator.

"What's going on?" They peeked out from inside the elevator, stopping the door too see who was coming toward them.

"Allen, hurry, we have to eat before the restaurant closes." Allen walked into the elevator seeing Amir standing near the floor panel. Upon seeing him Allen remembered meeting meeting him with Tim.

"I forgot to meet up with Jim, getting caught up with the excitement of being here. Only one day has passed but so much happened. It's good for me to enjoy what's around me, but I still have to remember what I came here for."

Allen thought as the elevator stopped at the dining room floor. The group rushed about grabbing the same breakfast choices as the day before. They all sat at the same table rapidly exchanging war stories. An Australian couple asked to sit with them. Allen told the Thai girls how he was set up while going to the different places on the tour. The Thai girls nodded in agreement. Amir told Allen that John had run the same scheme on him three days ago; designing a trip similar to the one he took yesterday. Allen had gotten away with the lowest price. Charlene and Tasanee had agreed to pay nearly triple what Allen had agreed to.

The Life and Times of Allen Court

The Australian woman put her two cents in; saying how the day before; she had her purse stolen from the taxi. The cab driver was the only one around.

"But he denied the whole thing." She said angrily with her boyfriend shaking his head confirming her.

"Yeah, and the next day I went to John and he said he would give us a new taxi driver. I told him that we were through with traveling with his drivers. We're moving to another hotel, today. We decided to go out on our own."

"Yeah, speaking of… Allen, you want to go out with us?" Charlene asked. Allen nodded, yes.

"I'm going with you. Forget Sal, it's no telling what might happen to me today with him."

They left the dining room hall for the elevator.

When they reached the bottom floor, John and Sal stood in front of the reception desk, waiting for Allen. The girl began ranting at Allen.

"You've left this man waiting for an hour, for you, that's an extra fifty dollars."

Allen looked past her, turning his attention to John.

"Hey, I'll be back at four o'clock. We can get the card then. Today, I'm going out with them." Amir, the two Thai girls with the Australian couple stood behind him.

"I'll see you later at four." Allen turned leading the temporary tourist strike. When they reached the parking lot they discussed their plan.

"We're going to go to the Egyptian Tower." Tasanee said confidently.

"How are we gonna get there?" Allen wondered.

"We're taking the subway." Amir told him. "For the last two days I have been using it. It's crowded, but we can get around." Amir led the way, taking them to the railway station. Allen looked at the old, rusty building, thinking "Is anything new here?" The girls stopped in a terminal surrounded by praying Muslims on a green carpet.

"Today is the first day of Ramadan." The Australian man said as Amir looked over his map. They stood in a lobby that had no working lights. The sun's rays cast the only light, as they bought tickets from the cashiers.

Amir led them to an underground station. They waited only a moment before the train arrived. The train sped across. From top to bottom, it was caked with so much dust that it was nearly black. People were packed shoulder to shoulder on the train. Traveling alone, on the Egyptian subway looked intimidating. The people rushed off the dusty train car. The car itself was large with old metal seats. The Arabic people stared at them as they plotted out their stops.

The Australian couple left the train one stop before them, taking their belongings to another hotel.

"Okay, we can get out here and walk to the tower." Amir told them. When the car came to a stop, they left the train and fell in line. Reaching the top of the stairs they were greeted by a wild commotion. Allen heard loud shouts around him as he began to make sense of the situation. Ahead of him, a large group of young people threw their hands up and marched towards a 3-story, cream-colored building.

"That's the American University of Cairo," Allen thought, as the students shouted in Arabic. He turned to his left, police in full riot gear stepped out of army trucks, holding shields and batons, lining in formation. Allen looked directly across the street from the police. Men stood standing in front of the stores, praying, shoulder to shoulder, arms outstretched palms upwards, barefooted, on a green carpet that stretched around the entire block. Allen turned back to the students. Some angrily protested, while a few others began setting fires. The men that were to his back on the prayer mat, stood calmly, praying out loud. The police began heading for the rioters. "I got to get out of Cairo!" Allen thought, as Amir stood with his jaw wide open.

"You thinking what I am thinking?" Allen asked Amir with him nodding.

"We need to leave. Come on, the bridge is this way," Amir said, they followed. Allen began walking contemplating his Egypt visit.

"I have to make sure Cynthia is all right," Allen thought as the group neared the bridge.

They walked across, Allen could see the Lotus Tower that they where headed for. Even with the cars whizzing by, he could still hear the rioting students. Allen began to voice his fears with Charlene.

"Before going any further I need to make some phone calls. I have to make sure my girls okay." Charlene nodded, understanding Allen's apprehension.

"That is right! You're an American. I almost forgot!" Her eyes widened. She grabbed Allen's hands tightly. "We must get you out of Cairo!" Allen looked down at the little woman and began laughing.

"That's cute. Could you do that again? I want to take picture." Allen pulled his camera out his bag. Charlene stood looking at him angrily.

"I'm serious! We must take you to your embassy." Click, the camera sounded as he took a picture. "Stop taking pictures of me!"

Click. "Tasanee!" Charlene yelled, catching up with Tasanne as she walked with Amir.

"I cant believe you Allen, you aren't serious!"

"My bad, it was just funny for a moment but if you like I will get real nervous and see if that does any good." He said cynically. Charlene huffed and walked off leaving the group. Allen caught up with her trying to make amends.

"I apologize, I just don't see how getting scared is going to help this situation. Don't worry about me. Just do what you came to do. I'll be alright."

They crossed the bridge and headed for the tower. Allen and Amir decided not to go up the tower. A man came by trying to sell fake papyrus posters.

"Those are banana, you can tell by the smell." Amir told Allen. Allen recognized one of the same posters he had bought the day before. This man was only asking for a tenth, of what the men at the shop had asked.

"Man, I spent ninety dollars at the "Papyrus Museum" …it's just a novelty spot." Admitted Allen.

Amir shook his head sadly.

"They got me for two hundred dollars. Charlene and Tasanee were the smartest of us all, they didn't buy anything." Amir told him. "But they more than made up for it at the carpet university." Amir added. They both began to laugh. "It's all negotiable."

"I was upset about it at the time, but now I can laugh about it. Once, I put it in perspective." Allen told him. "It's part of the experience of being here."

The girls returned from the tower.

"That was fun. You should have come up." Tasanee said to them. Allen's thoughts were in another place.

"With all that is going on, it's hard for me to relax. My friend, Cynthia, goes to school, right where they're rioting."

"I understand." Charlene said. "Is she there now?"

"No. She left for Aswan a few days before I arrived. I know I got to quit playing around and get to her."

The Life and Times of Allen Court

They walked across the bridge turning away from the university. The girls stopped to get a cup of orange juice. Allen stopped at a payphone. He called the two phone numbers he had for Cynthia. No answer from either one. "Well, she told me to call once I get to Aswan. I'm going one way or another."

He turned to see Amir and Tasanee drinking a cup of orange juice. He bought a glass for himself.

"Tasanee, you said you were going to a Mosque? Which one was it again?"

"The Mosque of Muhammad. We're going to take a cab over. You want to come?"

"Yeah, I would like to. What about you Amir?" Allen asked with Amir shaking his head in the negative.

"This is my last day here. I have to go back to the hotel and prepare for my flight."

"Thanks for the directions today," Allen told him. The girls gave Amir long hugs. He started walking back in the direction of the subway, while the girls waved for a cab. After five minutes of negotiating, they talked the cab driver down from twenty dollars to four. Allen referenced his To Go book, reading up on the mosque.

The Mosque of Muhammad was built by one of the conquering leaders. Within the book he was reading it stated that Cairo was once called Babylon before the Muslims reign. The Arab invaders were the last great wave of conquerors who took control of Cairo in 624 A.D. Allen looked out the window as the cab driver slowed near on a sloping road. The streets were filled with men in and women in flowing white robes. The cab driver dropped them off in front of a towering gray building. The ledges and windows looked exactly as one piece that had been carved out of stone. Allen pointed to the silent walls when they exited the cab.

They walked up the hill. At the highest peak, stood the mosques huge, sand- colored gates. A vast amount of neat well-trimmed grass surrounded the mosque. The place was in utter serenity, as groups of people walked along the tarred pathway to the gates, in awe of the view.

Upon entering the gates, Allen could see a long pathway. They walked along this brick path. The mosque reminded Allen of a fortress. After walking along, they came across the praying portion of the mosque. Removing their shoes, trading them for slippers, they went inside the temple. Some people prayed as other tourist looked around in wonder at the colorful massively connected art designs that expanded from one side of the floor to the concave of the ceiling and then back to the floor again.

Allen turned to point out a design to Charlene and noticed that they had left. He walked outside to see them standing in front of the enclosed tomb, taking pictures. He took one with them knowing that their time together was coming to an end.

"I have to get back to the hotel. I can't take the chance of missing out on getting my card back." The girls agreed, grabbed their shoes and began walking with him throughout the rest of the mosque.

"I know that it's later than four. Let's find a cab, quick" They walked along the streets for minutes before finding a cab driver. They didn't have to do much negotiating, but ended up stuck in standstill traffic. Allen sat in the front seat with Charlene and Tasanee in the back. The car nudged only inches ahead per minute. "I need to calm down," Allen thought. "I need some music," he flipped through his camera bag finding a CD. Allen held the CD up to the cab driver.

"Is it okay?' The cab driver nodded. "You'll like this," he told them. Allen let the rap music play as he bobbed his head along. Charlene and Tasanee moved along to the rhythm as the cab driver focused on the song. Allen waited for his favorite verse to kick in. Going along with the music; the girls stopped, in shock as the cabby stared on. Allen lifted his hands, matching the words. When he finished the girls started clapping.

"That was very great. I like that!" Charlene exclaimed still clapping.

"I really like that music. It's like nothing I have ever heard before." the cab driver told him. The car began to move ahead. Allen flipped through a number of songs finding other cuts that they would appreciate. They reached the hotel, the time 'flying by.' Allen walked into the lobby; Sal was sitting along the sofa watching television. The "good morning" receptionist began to lay into Allen.

"Where have you been? Do you know this man has waited here all afternoon for you?" The receptionist "spat out" her venom. "I can't believe you. We should charge you fifty dollars for this!"

"Didn't you try that this morning?" Allen questioned her calmly. "It didn't fly then; it's not going to fly now? Sy." Allen turned his attention to Sal.

"You ready to go?" Allen said to Sal. Sal stood up, not saying a word.

"When I get back, I'll most definitely say goodbye to you two." The girls headed for the elevator as Allen and Sal walked to the car. They quietly drove off from the hotel. They rode along in silence until; they reached an intersection that was packed with cars.

"I will have to take the highway." Sal said, turning off the road; nearly running into another dented Mercedes.

"No wonder these cars are on their last leg," thought Allen. They passed by the same faded billboard with the smiling Arabic woman. A swarm of cars ahead of them, made their ride to come to a halt. Huge groups of people were walking alongside the street protesting.

"What's going on?" Allen said aloud breaking his silence. "I saw a riot earlier today."

"Yes, things have been getting out of hand lately. People have been doing bad things, and hurting each other. But it's wrong. These are different times. People don't want or need war. People want to live. Have a good life." Allen thought about his comments as the car stopped at the bank. The sun was setting, turning the bright day into a muggy night.

Allen and Sal neared the door, where a lone guard stood out front. They had gotten there too late. The bank had closed.

"Ahhh, no!"

"Wait, right here." Sal began talking with the guard; it soon escalated into a shouting match. The guard went inside and to Allen's surprise, came back with the bank manager. Sal explained the situation to the manager. The bank manager asked Allen for proof of identity with Allen handing over his passport. The manager went into his office, returning minutes later with Allen's bank card.

"Minor miracles do happen every now and then," Allen thought, thanking the manager. Then he thanked Sal. He put his card into his wallet. After talking with the other travelers in the morning Allen had planned on being more responsible for the rest of his trip.

"I know where I can take you to exchange money." Sal told him. They stopped at a large hotel. "This is the place. I'll wait here." Allen went in taking out money from his account. He paid Sal for the day before, and gave him a tip for getting his card back.

"He's not a bad dude," Allen concluded, as they arrived at the hotel. Allen left the car, saying goodbye to Sal. He waited for his usual cold greeting by the receptionist. This time, she smiled at him.

"What's going on here?" Allen began to get worried.

"John is waiting for you in the dining hall upstairs." She told him politely.

"That game again, huh? I'm going there now." He rode up the elevator to meet John. The elevator stopped. Charlene and Tasanee walked by.

"Hi, Allen. Did you get your card back?" Charlene asked.

"I did."

"That's good." Tasanee broke in. "So will you be leaving soon?"

"Soon as I get my ticket. I'm about to see John now. You want to come to the dining room hall?" The girls nodded. Allen saw John sitting at the far end of the lunch room, overlooking the street. Allen walked closer; he could see the train lined up in the station only two hundred meters away.

"Hello, John." John put out the cigarette he was smoking holding his hand out for Allen to sit down. He took a seat with Tasanee and Charlene sitting on his left and right.

"You got your card back?" John asked calmly.

"Yes, I got it back." He stared at John intensely trying to read him. Allen gave him credit. John had a seasoned poker face.

"I got to tell you after going out today I know how much cheaper things are if you go about it yourself. I can't take your trip."

"What? You have already used up two days of my cab drivers time, as well as I have already bought the ticket for Aswan for you." John said with just enough conviction to let him know he was not taking it lightly.

"I paid Sal for his time yesterday. Today, we didn't go anywhere. I'll give you the money for the ticket and then we will be even."

"Okay, forget the money for the cab. But, I need money for a cancellation fee."

"What! A cancellation fee?" Allen questioned him. What type of story is he about to give me?

"See here. I have already written this down on paper. This paper cost money to replace this slip."

"The lies you tell for a dollar. I'm not going to pay you a cancellation... whatever, for a receipt." The Thai women broke in.

"No, no. Allen, you must catch your train! Don't worry, we will pay for it." Charlene motioned to him.

"No!" Allen said quickly to Charlene. "He has been playing us since the moment we stepped in this hotel he can at least do the right thing now." Allen told her as John calmly lit a cigarette.

"I'll pay for the ticket. How much are you letting it go for?" Allen asked.

"Fifty dollars." John said.

"We are in Egypt, talk to me in Egyptian pounds. Forget it! I'm going to give you fifty Egyptian pounds for it!" Allen told him.

"One hundred." John responded.

"Fifty-five." Allen bartered.

"Ninety. Or else, you will not have your ticket for Aswan."

"Sixty pounds. Or you'll be stuck with a ticket you have paid for and now can't use." Stalemate. Allen had blown John's cover; he could see him getting angry with him. They now sat stared at each other not saying a word. The Thai women tried to calm the situation, but neither one of the men were paying attention. John stalled for a moment breathing in a hale of cigarette smoke eyeing him through the thin gray whiffs.

"My last offer is sixty five pounds." The train whistle blew. John took one last puff of his cigarette.

193

"I have never had this happen." He put the cigarette down in the ashtray. "I'll accept it."

The Thai girls clapped again, as they all left the table.

"I'll help you with your bags when you come downstairs," John told him. Allen hugged Charlene and Tasanee.

"Thank you for all of your help."

"We liked walking around with you." Tasanee told him while on the elevator. They reached the floor with bottom floor with Allen grabbing his luggage. He took his suitcase and his downstairs to see a group of Arabic men standing around the front desk with John. Allen walked over to the counter. He waved goodbye to the receptionist. He turned to John.

"John, you ready?" John turned picking up Allen's suitcase and led the way to the train station, getting there in minutes. Allen stepped along the ancient hulk of a train.

"Here's your ticket to Aswan. The seats are very large." John stepped on the train walking him to his seat. Allen placed his things in an overhead compartment.

"Have a safe trip." John told him, shaking his hand.

"Thanks." Allen watched him walk out. I can't take it personal; it may just be business for them. Allen took a seat by the window. After a few moments, the train pulled off. Ten hours to Aswan, ten hours to Cynthia.

*

Allen looked into the Nile River; he glanced out the window seat. Silver reflections bounced off the water as the train rolled down the track. After leaving the city, Allen noticed that the train was near the river and had continued following it for the last three hours. "Seven more left," he thought as his stomach stirred hungrily. "It's like I'm starting everything all over again." His eyes wandered over the passing trees. "I made a reservation at another hotel just in case I don't get a hold of Cynthia soon enough." The train continued moving at a snails pace. The slow drum of the rail-cars wheels only added to his restlessness. Arabic men sat and had long, amplified conversations with one another.

"If I didn't have on these clothes, I probably could blend in. But with these clothes, sneakers and all, I'm recognized instantly, as a foreigner." He thought adjusting his seat, leaning it backwards. "Forget it; let me take my mind off this." He closed his eyes, falling asleep.

~

He awoke with a jolt, as the train pulled off from another station waking him up. He looked out the window; the sun had claimed the moons place. The sun cast a thousand reflections across the Nile's water. Balm trees swayed peacefully in front of the Nile, representing life, in the desert valleys. Allen looked at the sight... his first thoughts were as silent as his breath.

The desert floated in the background. The Nile River shone like glass through the light of the dawning sun. A feeling of being close to heaven began to enter his mind. "How much longer till Aswan? Maybe, other two or three hours he thought resting.

An hour later, the train pulled into one of its last stations. A few people left the car as a small number of new people boarded. After sometime, Allen heard a man speaking humbly in English. He turned to see a thin, Nubian man in white linen clothing, standing a little over five feet tall. The Nubian man tried talking to two European tourists, unsuccessfully. They shook their heads, not interested. "I wonder if this is one of the hotel people that I heard about trying to get you to book a room. The man walked near his seat, stopping close to him.

"Hello, my brother, I wanted to know if you needed a boat to ride along the Nile? I am a felucca captain." Allen remembered what Cynthia had told him.

"Those are the little boats that Cynthia had told me about." The man dug in his pocket showing him a piece of laminated paper.

"See, this is a review of my boat." He handed it to Allen. Allen read it over. A travel writer had happened to take the ride. The writer said that his experience with Captain Thomas was an enjoyable one.

"I'm, Captain Thomas." The little Nubian man said proudly. "My trip will take three days. You will sleep and eat on the boat, that's if you so choose to come. It cost's seventy Egyptian pounds. We will make stops at Kom Ombo and the temple of Edfu. Food is included, but I suggest you bring your own water. If you want, you can have a free ride to Elephantine Island, after we reach Aswan. Then if you like, you can pay thirty five pounds that day and pay the other half upon completion of the trip." Allen nodded his head in agreement. The man appeared humble and knowledgeable about his boat. The trial run would help Allen fully decide.

"You can meet me at the dock at six." The captain told him.

"I have a friend waiting for me in Aswan wanting to take the trip up the river to Karnak. If she wants to go, then, we'll ride together, if it's cool with you?" Captain Bob nodded. Allen shook his hand; Bob walked onto another train car.

*

It took him only twenty minutes to find his hotel. He used the lobby phone to call Cynthia. Allen began to write a brief note to her that turned into a letter. It took another twenty minutes, before he could dial the number.

"This time, it's for real," he thought. Putting his fingers on the dial pad; Cynthia picked up on the first ring.

"Cynthia, hey."

"Allen!" Her voice reflected her excitement. "I'm so glad you made it!"

"It wasn't easy, but yeah, I'm finally here."

"Did you enjoy yourself, in Cairo?"

"It was eye-opening, to say the least. Dealing with shady salesman and seeing all the old tombs, it was a lot to take in. I even met one of those felucca captains you were telling me about. He was telling me about staying on board for the next three days."

"Oh," She said disappointed.

"What do you mean, "Oh"?" Allen asked.

"Well, I was hoping that you would be able to spend some time here with me."

"No doubt." Allen told her. "I was just thinking that we could cruise on the same boat together for the next three days."

"I would love to, but I still haven't finished the research assignment. I may have to stay here a little longer then I expected."

"Well, can you meet me at the boat dock at six o'clock? The felucca captain did say we could have a free trip to Elephantine Island."

"Yeah, I can meet you there later. It's good hearing from you, Allen."

"Yeah, I'll see you soon." He told her.

"Decision time," Allen thought putting down the receiver. Should I keep traveling and getting into what I can, or, should I hold tight and spend some time? I didn't come all this way for nothing. If she's the one, it's gonna show." He returned to his room, finding pen and paper. He began to write out all the words he had found it hard for him to tell Cynthia. "After all this time…how will she respond to this?" I'll know soon enough."

~

It took him a few minute to find the boat. He stood at the top of the boat dock, watching the other passengers' board. He waited nervously, wondering, how she would look after nearly two years. He watched a slender figure approach, his jaw dropped. Cynthia was there before him. She was wearing a thin, olive-colored, summer dress. In his eyes, everything but the water stopped moving. She glided up and kissed him on the cheek.

"You are looking, more than fine." He pulled her towards him and hugged her tightly.

"I missed you too much." She told him, looking into his eyes. "It's been along time."

"Too long," he told her. "Look. You've always said you like the words that I write to you; so, I have something to give you. I want you to read it. And…just tell me how you feel." He handed her a letter. She stood for minutes reading it, thinking turning the words over in her heart. The word that stood out, just so happened to be the first word, on the page. "Today."

"Something in your eyes tells me that it, that we're about to change." Allen told her.

"It already has." Cynthia kindly told him, at that moment, the felucca captain called out to Allen.

"You still want to take that trip?" Cynthia asked him? Allen looked down to the boat dock and waved to the captain goodbye.

"Right now, I have better things to do." He hugged her again.

"What's that?" She asked with a smile upon her face.

"That's, being with you. You want to go for a walk?" Allen asked.

Cynthia took his hand.

"I do."

*

Allen told Cynthia of the scheming salesmen in Cairo and the girls he had dated up North. None of the things seemed to faze her. She had been through her own list of shady salesmen and bad relationships. They seemed to be writing on opposite ends of the same page.

Allen spoke of new friends he had made and some plans he had for their future together. She told him about her research project, building new living centers in this country. How the children were so poor, that their only toys were pen and paper. She also schooled him on a few local things, concerning the food and customs. She had a new nickname, Kemet.

They took many walks around town before settling down in her apartment in the city. The thought of traveling other places had been tempting to Allen; but compared to the time he had now with Cynthia, it was all an afterthought. He was glad to be with someone he had known and trusted for so long in his life. Their connection was still strong.

"One day we can travel together. That is, when we get enough money." Allen told her, as Cynthia chuckled.

"That may be sooner than you think. When are you going home?" Cynthia asked.

"In two or three weeks, I'll fly back."

The Life and Times of Allen Court

"I have to go the week after and settle some things. Just some money matters." She said quietly. "I want to spend as much time as possible with you, if it's all right?"

"You know it is."

~

For a while, Allen forgot about the trip to Elephantine Island and the visit to the Karnak temples. He was far too busy worshipping at the temple of 'Kemet.' He spent much of his time reacquainting himself with Cynthia. They talked for hours, laughing and sometimes arguing, but mostly, making up for lost time. They spoke of many things, and enjoyed each others company. He slept a while and had many dreams while lying beside her. One of them stood out in his mind.

*

And in the dawn, he stood underneath a tree, "the size of creation." The sun glowed in white and gold elliptical spheres around the edges of one-large-shaped leaf. The leaf floated directly above him, in the center of the sun's light. The leaf grew large within the vision; he saw the branches reconnecting back to the tree; the sun cast its brilliance behind it. A voice, unlike anyone he had ever known, yet familiar, spoke to him.

"And like a branch from this tree, you are a part of the life hanging from the vines, for all your moments are but memories, blessed are the ones you hold now." He rose from his sleep, waking Cynthia from hers. He then asked her to marry him. She said, "Yes."

~

Epilogue:

Flying home, Allen was losing badly to an eleven year old in a game of Tunk.

"I think you've cheated me," He joked.

"No, it's just in the cards. Maybe, you will win the next hand?"

"Same bet, or double or nothing," Allen asked?

"If you lose, you'll owe me two candy bars." The kid was serious. Allen thought for a moment.

"All right, I can risk it."

The kid pulled a card dropping two aces leaving Allen holding a king. The girl laughed aloud. Allen handed the kid her prize. A handful of candy.

"These are my favorite." She looked at him curiously. "How did you know?"

"My favorite too!" This satisfied the kid. She ate one happily. Allen looked at the clouds around him. He ended up leaving Egypt two weeks after Cynthia. In the end, he did get a chance to see the Karnak and Luxor temples, the Valley of the Kings and many other sites. He had continued on eastward leaving Egypt but now was the time to return home. Thinking of the history of the places he had been; he felt that he was living some never-ending life. He had begun to follow his instinct, what some would say the first mind.

Before he stepped on the plane, he stopped at kiosk store in the airport. The cashier had looked at him odd, when he had bought so much candy at her register.

"Got a sweet tooth?" She asked, Allen nodded.

"It's for a friend." The girl shook her head and busied herself with another customer. Allen moved on. On the plane, the flight attendant handed out the newspapers. It seemed that after a five-month wait a foreign-exchange student had turned in her winning lottery ticket. Allen smiled as he read over the headlines.

"Hey, you got more!" The kid asked, "We can play again?"

"I only have some left but; I have to save it for someone." Allen told her.

The plane began to descend. After a walk through customs, Allen stood at the baggage gate waiting for his bride to be. Cynthia walked in, Allen handed her a small gift of chocolate.

"Is this for me? How do you know, what I like?" She laughed.

"I just remembered." He said.

When they walked out the door; for some reason Allen thought of the vision he had the day before leaving to Finland. It was a dream that awakened him from a deep sleep. Finally, he grasped its true meaning.

"I finally know…" he paused for a moment, "…what the gift is." He told her.

"What is it?" She asked. He looked at her before responding.

"Love."

*